JUST LIKE GREY 14

VICTOR ROUSSO

JESSIE COOKE

WWW.JESSIECOOKE.COM

CONTENTS

A Word from Jessie   v

Chapter 1	1
Chapter 2	14
Chapter 3	20
Chapter 4	30
Chapter 5	41
Chapter 6	46
Chapter 7	50
Chapter 8	58
Chapter 9	62
Chapter 10	68
Chapter 11	75
Chapter 12	79
Chapter 13	86
Chapter 14	96
Chapter 15	101
Chapter 16	107
Chapter 17	113
Chapter 18	119
Chapter 19	124
Epilogue	129

More Books by Jessie Cooke   133

A WORD FROM JESSIE

Just like Grey is an Amazon Best Selling Series.

All books in the series are written for open-minded adults who are not easily offended, so you will encounter anything from cheating, explicit sex, unprotected sex, drug use, adult language, and many more topics that could upset the wrong reader.

These are not vanilla stories.

That said...I hope you enjoy it.

Happy Reading,

Jess

1

VICTOR

As I looked down, out of the plane window, and upon the idyllic scenery of the French countryside below, I couldn't help but smile.

I was glad to be back.

France had always been my second home. Maybe even more than America ever had been. My parents had tried to make sure we grew up somewhere a little more multicultural, somewhere we could use as a jumping-off point for the rest of our lives, but I always found myself drawn back here. And I wasn't sure it was ever going to change. As far as I was concerned, this place was my home, and I was glad to be back.

"Are we almost there?" Oliver asked, yawning and stretching beside me as he rubbed the tiredness away from his eyes. I nodded.

"Nearly," I replied. Even though this was such a long flight, I couldn't find it in me to rest at all. I was too excited to get to France once more. I knew Oliver made this trip a few times a year, so it wasn't nearly as exciting to him, but to me, this was everything I had been waiting for, and I was going to enjoy every moment of it.

It had all started when I had figured it was time to do something with my life. Something that didn't just involve kicking around New York with my brothers and the rest of my family; now that the two of them seemed to have settled down and found women they wanted to spend the rest of their lives with, I was the last one left without someone to call my own. And hell, in lieu of a girl, I could at least find a business that spoke to me, couldn't I?

I had done a little research, digging around until I found something that interested me…a vineyard, back in Brittany, the North of France, where it was a little cooler in the winter and a little more colorful in the summer. It was run by Oliver Moreau and his wife, Natalie, whom I had yet to meet; she stayed out in France all year round, just to keep an eye on things on the ground, and I was probably far more jealous of her than I ever should have been.

The plane came to a halt on a small strip of tarmac not far from the mountains. The jet we'd taken across the Atlantic was a private one, so I didn't have to worry about waiting around for a stack of people to pour off in front of me, much to my relief. I wanted nothing more than to climb out of this place and inhale a great big lungful of the French air, bring myself back home again, and this time, find some excuse to never leave.

I stepped out of the plane and on to the stairs that had been brought out for us, and smiled as soon as I looked around. It was a little colder here than it had been in New York, but I didn't mind. I would have put up with a blizzard if it meant I could just enjoy being here once more. My mother had fussed over me going, told me that the very least I could do was send dozens of pictures so my father could reminisce about coming here himself, and I had promised her I was going to do my very best to deliver. I pulled out my phone and snapped a couple of images of the mountains before me. I would have to put aside a day to climb them when I got the chance. I didn't want to miss out on a second of this place.

New York had never really felt like home to me. It was all too urban, a side of life that had never really appealed to me, if I was being honest. It was clean-cut and neatly packaged, and I wanted something that felt a little wilder. Something that opened me up to things I might not ever have considered before.

"You should get some rest," Oliver remarked to me, as he came down the stairs behind me. "You want to be in full fighting form by the time we get down to work tomorrow."

"I will," I promised him, but I knew it was a lie. I'd be up all night, trying to plan everything I wanted to do while I was here. I knew I should have been focused on just what I had promised to take care of while I was with him, but hey, it would have been rude to come all the way over to France and not make the most of every moment of it, right?

"Good," Oliver yawned. "Now, if you'll excuse me, I'm going to see my wife. I think the driver will already be there with the car to take you to the hotel..."

I nodded, and he slapped me on the shoulder before he brushed past me and headed down the stairs towards the woman he hadn't seen in weeks. I knew it must have been hard for them, being apart for this long, but it must have made the coming-together again even more fun, right?

I grinned as I headed to my car. That was one of the things I had always loved the very most about France. I'd lost my virginity here when I was a teenager, and I swear, it was like my sexuality had lived in this place ever since. Whenever I returned, I would find myself seeking out that which I might have not been interested in back home. Not that I didn't like everything New York had to offer in the way of women, but France, and Brittany, in particular...it was a beautiful place, and the women seemed to approach life with a vivaciousness that American women often lacked.

Though I was mostly intrigued to find out what the scene was like down here. Not just the dating scene...no, I already had a good grasp of that, but the kink scene. I had been involved with it for a few years now, since I bit the bullet and found a way into a gathering when I turned thirty. It had been something I'd been interested in for a long time, but I'd never known how the hell I was meant to approach it without just making a total fucking fool of myself, so I had avoided it for as long as I could bear before I decided to give it a shot.

And damn...it was everything I had been looking for. Almost enough to make me believe that the city could have been enough for me, if I just gave it the chance. I knew it was a long shot, but the life it gave me, that it injected into my veins, it was electric. I had never found a woman who I had been interested in playing with long-term, but perhaps I would be able to find one here. And, if I did, I was sure I was going to get addicted in moments.

I had done a little research into everything France had to offer, spoken to a few people who had come out here to play and what they had found, and everything they had told me had tantalized me beyond a point that I could handle it. I knew there was so much for me to uncover, so much for me to learn, and I just had to choose where I was going to start.

In fact, that was how I had met Oliver, how I had come across his business when I did. He had been at one of the meet-ups I'd attended, and, once I'd noticed his accent, I had started chatting with him about his time in France. Not only did we have an interest in this stuff in common, he had the perfect business for me to invest in. We had become fast friends not long after that, and I knew I would never have to worry about getting exposed involved in something he didn't approve of – since he was up to his neck in it himself.

But for now, I knew Oliver was right. I needed to get some sleep so I could be fighting fit for the next day. I had no idea what the next few weeks were going to bring; I had a couple of months here before I was returning home once more, and I knew I wanted to make the very most of it I could.

The hotel was expensive. Oliver and his wife had made plenty of money with their vineyard, which was why they were looking for investors like me to expand on it, but I hardly noticed as I headed up the velvet-lined stairs towards my room. The woman at the desk smiled at me widely, and I smiled right back at her. Because I was back home, back where I belonged. And I knew there was nothing that could take the joy of this feeling away from me. I was going to enjoy every second of it I could and that started right here, right now.

JUST LIKE GREY 15:

Victor Rousso...sample

"How many dicks do we need?" Heather said. She lugged two brown cardboard boxes as the front door closed with a whoosh.

"A bigger shop means more merchandise," Kristal said.

"You just better hope that we'll get more customers to buy it." Heather let the box drop on the top of the brand-new glass case with a heavy thud, and Kristal ripped her apple lollipop from her mouth and cringed.

"Hey!" Kristal said. "You'll break the display case."

"What do I care?" Heather said dramatically. "My back aches from lugging in all these boxes. Who thought it was a good idea to tell the delivery man to leave them outside the door?"

"You did," Kristal said. "Because your choice of men forced us to flee our old shop into this venue for our sex toys..."

Heather frowned.

"Darn gossipy delivery men. Who'd have thought they'd be worse than women?"

Kristal bit into her lip. If it hadn't been for an overly chatty delivery man that Heather flirted with, they wouldn't have had to move from their cheaper Chinatown location. Mr. Chatty told Heather of a man asking questions about Kristal that sent them into flight mode. Now they had to keep a low profile, and so any shop they had could not allow free-roaming public entry. The implements of intimate pleasures they hawked provided a perfect excuse to set up a shop that only allowed admission by invitation. Hence the shop's name: Shop By Invitation Only or Shop—BIO for short.

"It is not a sex toy shop," Heather said emphatically.

"Right. Because we don't sell dildos, flavored lube, and edible panties."

Heather pulled a cardboard cutter from her pocket and sliced open the box with a quick jerk of her arm.

"Hence my question, Miss Frost." She pulled out a bubble-wrapped nine-inch dildo and waved it in Kristal's face. "How many of these things did you order? We have enough dick here to keep us busy for a year."

"No sampling the merchandise," Kristal said. She snatched the sex toy from Heather's hand.

"Yeah, yeah. What do you expect me to do since you made me break up with the delivery man?" She ripped open the second box.

"Point of order," Kristal said. "I did not *make* you break up with him."

"I'm pretty sure that threatening to hide all my vibrating condoms constituted a threat."

"One. You did not pay for those. I repatriated them for the good of the store. Two—"

Heather put her hand on her hip. "Two what?"

"It's too damn bad he wasn't good enough for you." She waited a moment to gauge Heather's reaction. The fact was that despite Heather's flirts, Mr. Yappity Yap wouldn't move the needle to ask Heather out. When Heather became too obvious, he mumbled something about not picking up girls in sex shops and hightailed it out of the shop.

"Damn straight, he wasn't good enough. That's why I asked the delivery people to send someone else."

"You did not. We're in a different part of the city now. There would be a different person. But no hitting on the delivery men, okay? It's getting expensive to move storefronts."

"Yeah, yeah," Heather said. "A stone's throw away from Times Square."

"A Fifth Avenue address."

"Yes," Heather said in a droll tone. "Where all the riff-raff live."

"You mean the filthy rich."

"Their dirty secrets are our livelihood."

Kristal rolled her eyes. "When and if we get them for customers. We have a lot of work to do to get there."

"Work, work, work." Heather sighed as she ripped open the second box.

"*Fifty Shades?*" Heather said incredulously. "Why did you order that?" The derision in her voice sliced like a knife.

"It's only five copies, and it's a popular book."

"It does not accurately reflect the practice or the community. Here..." She pulled a black lacy bustier from another box. "Try this on. It looks like your size." She tossed it to Kristal.

"We're supposed to sell the merchandise and not wear it."

"Sweetheart, to sell the merchandise we have to show it off. Now put it on."

Kristal sighed but took off her shirt and bra with her back to Heather, though her roommate had seen her in the altogether many times. It just seemed weird to put it on there.

"Anyway, the book sparked conversation about BDSM, and suddenly spanking wasn't a deviant act."

"I don't know. Men paid good money to get spanked. Now they can go to their girlfriends for it."

"So sorry, Miss Domme," Kristal said, "but you were ready to put aside your profession. When I suggested opening a shop, you jumped at it like those frou-frou dogs jump through hoops in the circus."

Heather put her hand on her hip and gave Kristal her best Domme look. "Frou-frou dog?"

"If the analogy fits, wear it." Kristal glanced over her shoulder to catch Heather's reaction.

Heather laughed and shook her head. The magenta ends of her black hair shook with her merriment. "That's a good one."

Kristal hooked in the bustier and turned around. "How does it look?"

"Like you're ready for some fun."

"We'd better work or we won't be able to afford to have fun. Get cracking."

Instead Heather stared at a *Fifty Shades* from the shipment.

"What are you doing?" Kristal asked.

"Let's look at that oh-so-famous contract and see what Anna contemplated signing on to. Hmmm. There's spanking, paddling, whipping, caning, biting, nipple clamps, genital clamps, ice, hot wax on the list. Gee, and Mr. Grey was giving this juicy BDSM away? What's the fun in that?"

Kristal scoffed and snatched the book out of her business

partner's hand. "I'm sure that as an international billionaire, he didn't need the income."

"Seems like a missed opportunity to me. I thought the one percent had a rapacious appetite for money."

"You have the rapacious appetite for money. Okay, Miss Domme, would you charge for discipline?"

"It depends." She picked up a pen out of her purse and took the book again.

"Wait, what are you doing?"

Heather tapped the book with her pen. "A good paddling, fifty dollars." She scribbled in the book.

"Fifty dollars to get your ass whipped? That seems excessive."

Heather chuckled. "I assure you, they kept coming back for more. But you, sweetie, don't need to pay to get your sweet ass spanked. Men would line up for the privilege if you gave them the chance."

"What's next there?"

"Whipping—Hmm. Two hundred bucks to start."

"Two what?" Kristal said.

"Hey, whipping demands knowledge and skill. Use a whip wrong and you can cause severe bodily injury or even death. Same with caning, too."

"Good to know," Kristal said.

"Biting—ew, no. You never know someone's health status."

"True."

"Nipple clamps—$250."

"A guy would want nipple clamps?"

"Sure. Certain men get off on that level of pain. Genital clamps, yeah, since the liability is high there—$500."

"Doesn't that price men out of the market?"

"It would surprise you. Come on. Don't tell me that no one ever offered you genital clamps?"

"I'm not that experienced." Kristal had been too busy surviving in New York and didn't have time for fun and games. Heather had introduced her to one Dom, and she played with him for a while until she found out the rat was a married man. That soured the whole idea for her and she broke things off.

As if there could be a thing, she thought.

Heather kept up her murmurs. "Ice, on the house. I love to make a man shiver. Hot wax—ooh, that's fun, the way the wax drips on the body. How a man winces as the hot wax hits is simply delicious. Fifty dollars."

"Oh, my God. Fun for you, you sadist."

"Allow me my vices, woman. I allow you yours."

"I hardly think addiction to apple juice qualifies as co-equal debauchery."

"You're right. Mine are more fun."

"You," Kristal said, exasperated. "Go finish the order for Master William. He's expecting that handmade leather corset for his fiancée. You do not keep Master William waiting."

"If he wasn't such a good customer, I'd tell him he had to wait four weeks like everyone else."

"Hush. He's more than a good customer. He's one of our best distributors and he's an investor, which keeps us in lattes instead of on the street, so stop whining. Hop on it or I'll beat you with this huge specimen of fake manhood."

Heather stuck her tongue out at Kristal, and Kristal did her best to keep her expression stern, but she couldn't help it. And neither could Heather. They both broke out in giggles and couldn't stop laughing. Heather slapped her hand on the top of the glass counter, and Kristal braced herself on the wrapping station behind her as she desperately tried to calm her guffaws.

The doorbell rang, and with a last gasp of laughter that she tried to hold in, Kristal pressed the button for the intercom.

"William Ianucci," crackled the intercom.

Heather straightened and muttered, "Oh shit." She scrambled into the workroom.

"Great, leave me to the Dom to explain why his order isn't ready," called Kristal. She knew Heather heard her. But actually, Master William, despite his fierce Dom reputation, always showed respect to women. She buzzed the lock to release it and in walked the dungeon master of one of New York City's popular BDSM clubs, La Corda Rosa.

Master William's tall yet wiry body, combined with dark hair and blue eyes, gave him a commanding presence. His high cheekbones, aquiline nose, and perfectly straight posture lent him an aristocratic air. He wore a black leather jacket against New York's winter chill. This surprised her because he called it a cliché of the BDSM lifestyle.

"Hello, Master William. Good to see you again. Nice jacket."

"Nice bustier."

"Thanks. It just came in a shipment."

"Do you like my jacket? It was a birthday gift from my fiancée."

Ah, the famous Miss Samantha. Kristal had not yet met Master William's fiancée, and she was slightly jealous that another New York woman had found her dream man. Not the Kristal would go for William. She favored a more Ivy League look than William's Italian heritage. Somewhere there had to a man for her in a city filled with nearly five million men.

"She's a lucky woman."

William smiled, something Kristal was not used to. It made him even more charming. She wanted to learn the secret of his fiancée's hold on Master William to duplicate this mysterious Miss Samantha's success with another Dom.

"So," William said. "About business."

"I'm sorry. The corset is not ready yet."

"I didn't expect it to be." His face fell into the authoritative air she expected from him. "I have some orders and I wanted to go over the details with Miss Heather."

"Just a minute." She ducked into the backroom while Master William turned his attention to butt plugs she had set out on a display. "Oh, Miss Heather," she sing-songed. "Your favorite Dom is here to see you."

Heather swore, but she grabbed the dressmaker's dummy she had been using to craft the corset and dragged it into the store.

"Good to see you again, Master William."

"Likewise, Miss Heather." He flicked a glance at the corset. "Lovely. I'm sure it will be perfect, as usual."

"I'm sorry it's not ready."

"Not a problem. Just as long as it's finished by my next mixer, that will be fine. Miss Samantha will attend, and I want to show her off."

"When is that again?"

"Two weeks from today. You are coming, right?"

"Well…" Heather said. Her voice trailed off, and she turned her attention to the corset again and picked at a loose thread.

"Don't tell me you didn't receive an invitation?"

"I'm sure it is in the mail," Kristal said.

"I sent you both invitations. To tell you the truth, I know some Doms looking for good subs."

"That would be Kristal there," Heather said.

"Yes, Miss Heather is on the fence on whether to Top or Bottom." Heather rolled her eyes.

"Nothing wrong with being a Switch," William said. "Some male subs in my club would love to meet a new Domme."

Heather shrugged. "My experience with male subs—" She sighed.

"Don't sell yourself short, Miss Heather. Sometimes all it takes is meeting the right one. You are both more than welcome.

In fact, I expect you to be there. Let me check." He looked inside his jacket and then pulled out two yellow cards. "I have these extra invitations, so take these."

"Sure thing, Master William," Kristal said. She took the invitations and put them on the counter by the cash register.

"Have you eaten yet, ladies?"

"No," they said together, then Heather smirked.

"Well, go to Romallo's and collect your free opening day pizza."

"Master William, you've been too generous to us."

"What generous? It's one pizza. Go get it. I've already ordered it for you. You wouldn't want it to get cold."

Click here to read Just like Grey 15: Victor's story.

2

LAUREN

"Lauren, could you take the bottle of wine out to table three, please?" Marion, the head of kitchen staff, called to me as I hustled back through the door from my last journey out. I nodded, scooping up the carefully arranged selection on the silver tray that was waiting for me and doing my very best not to send it all crashing to the ground. That would somewhat break the appeal of the glamor of this place. Though, no doubt, somebody here would have a kink for it.

"On it!" I called back to her, and I turned and headed straight back out the door to take this down to the table that had requested it.

I knew some people would have found this line of work odd. It was one of the reasons, I had to assume, that I had been offered the job when I had next to no waitressing ability. I was more used to cooking in the kitchen, not rushing food back and forth out of it, but hey, they seemed happy with the work I did for them, and that was all that mattered.

Not that I made much of an effort to broadcast what I did in my evenings to anyone else. I knew all my American friends back home would have swooned on to their fainting couches and demanded smelling salts if they'd guessed for an instant that I was spending my time serving drinks to perverts, deviants, and other kink enthusiasts from all over France, in the most exclusive BDSM club in the country, Petit Mort.

And I supposed that some of the appeal of the place was knowing how crazy it would have driven a lot of the people that I had grown up with. It's natural to rebel when you get a little older. I know a lot of kids who would steal their parents' cars when they were teenagers, go for death drives around the suburbs at top speed in the middle of the night, trying to avoid taking out a mailbox on the way. What I did was far less dangerous, though I knew most of them would have hated it far more anyway.

But I didn't give a damn. This was what paid my bills, and I had learned more about the world and about myself working here than any of them had back home getting their third degrees because they couldn't think of anything better to do with their lives.

I had been twenty-one when I had run away from home for good. Just graduated cooking school, a pastry chef with a decent side-hustle catering for baptisms and bar mitzvahs, but I was getting bored. Antsy. I could see there was a whole world out there for me, and I couldn't help but wonder what it might have held. I was dating a boy my parents thoroughly approved of at the time, some kid named David, and I knew it wouldn't be long until he popped the question and I would have to pretend the thought of pumping out a few kids for him and settling down was the best thing that could ever have happened to me.

France was calling. I'm still not sure why I picked France, maybe just because it was the next flight that was leaving when I decided to go, but it made sense to me back then. And I hadn't regretted it for an instant, not since I had stepped off the place and looked around and known, known for sure this place was my home and that it was always going to be. I had left a note for David tucked through his mailbox slot, picked up a new phone, and changed my number so nobody could get in touch with me. My parents were beside themselves until I dropped them an email to let them know I was okay, though I'm pretty sure they were even angrier when they realized I had taken off and broken all the rules they had tried to instill into me over the years.

But they must have known, even when I was younger, that I was never going to fall in line with everything they wanted from me. I had always been restless, keen to see what the rest of the world had to offer, and now I was in France, I was never going to go back to what I had known before. I had a life here. It might not have been the life they had dreamed up for me way back in the day, but I didn't care. It was the one that suited me, down to the ground, and I wasn't going to give it up for anything.

I worked during the day as a pastry chef for a little coffee shop around the corner. It had been a nightmare at first, as I'd tried to learn French on the hop, but I had managed to pull myself together enough to be able to ask the customers about their husbands and their kids and generally get over their suspicion at a foreigner working in their small town. Renting a little apartment not far from the train station, I realized the cash I was bringing in baking wasn't going to be enough, so I started looking for something else...something I could really use to pay the bills.

It was a guy I had been seeing for a few weeks who had introduced me to the Mort. If I hadn't known it was there, I would just have wandered right past it, the nondescript place standing in the corner of two streets, a dark red door lined with deep wood that looked as though it should have belonged to some fancy lawyer or something like that. But inside there was more than I had ever expected.

I could still remember the first time I had come here, during the day, when everything was lit up and decidedly normal…well, as normal as things can be in a BDSM club, at least. I had never seen anything like it before in my life, and it was the strangest thing, seeing it all laid out for cleaning and tidying before the clientele returned for another evening of debauchery. Crosses with ties that were meant to trap the participants upon them, whips and chains and bindings to hurt and restrain, even these strange wands that lit up purple near the end and buzzed with electricity every time I was in hearing distance of it.

The place was made up of a few small booths, which could only have housed a half-dozen people at most each. They came equipped with their own selection of toys and other on-the-house gifts that could be used by anyone who came in. Leather seats and discreet dividers stained in the same dark wood as the door gave the people who were hiding in there their privacy, and, with the lights down and the dim redness spreading across the floor from the chandelier above, it looked like the most delicious version of hell that you could imagine.

I had never been into kink before I'd found out about this place. Okay, I'd allowed a few guys to spank me, had even been into a little hair-pulling and maybe some name-calling if I was feeling particularly dirty. But this place introduced me to stuff that I didn't even know people could have been into. The pain, the pleasure that I saw there every night, from people indulging their darkest and most twisted desires with their partners, it always fascinated me. And I would have been lying if I'd said I didn't go home most nights hot and bothered, feeling as though I was going to burst if I didn't find someone to work out my own desires with instead.

But it paid well, and I liked the people I was serving. Most of them paid a solid admission fee just to be allowed to return to this place on the regular, and they were carefully vetted for manners and their ability to respect the people they were playing with. I never had to worry about being snapped at or talked down to. In fact, I would say I got far more shit from the people I served at the bakery than I did down here, though nobody would ever have believed it.

That particular night, it was busy. There were a few new guests arriving today, and we were going out of our way to make sure they got the best service possible so they would keep coming back. They were only allowed a few drinks while they were actually playing, but if they were just observing the performers for the night, they could have as much as they wanted, and this particular table I was serving was making sure they kept the expensive booze coming.

They were watching the rope performers that evening. We had a small stage that was used to display artists in the BDSM world, and honestly, they were one of the coolest parts about working in this place. Before, I would never have thought I could be as taken with their talents as I was, but they were amazing, no doubt about it at all. The girls on the stage tonight were binding each other up in the most amazing concoctions. I was surprised they didn't tear something, either the rope or a muscle, but they seemed to have total control of everything that was going on. Good for them. If I had tried something like that, I would have been caught up in my own panties within seconds. I couldn't even step out of a pair of jeans without getting them caught around my waist, and I had no clue how they could pull something like that off...

The rest of the shift went relatively quickly, thanks in no small part to how busy it was in there that evening. By the time I was finished my night, I sat outside on the step, rubbing my feet before I had to take the cobbled streets back to my apartment.

I tipped my head back and looked at the sky above me. It was speckled with stars, a few obscured by clouds, but the moon was burning the majority of them away. It looked gorgeous. It was at times like this when I was totally glad I had decided to run away from the life I'd known before, even if I was sure that most of my family would never forgive me for it.

But it was worth it. I was happy, and I felt alive when I was here, alive in a way I knew I would never have been able to back home. It might have changed everything, but I was sure it had changed everything for the better, and nothing was going to convince me I had made the wrong choice escaping the drudgery of what was expected of me back there and taking on the thrill of everything I could down here.

I rose to my feet...time to go home. The only thing that could have made this any more perfect than it already was, would be if I had someone waiting for me who could rub my feet for me.

Or, you know, something a little more fun than that.

3

VICTOR

"This is what you've been waiting for, right, Victor?" Oliver remarked to me, as we made our way down the street and towards the club he had been talking up since the first night I met him. I nodded.

"I just want to see if this place actually exists or not," I teased him, and he chuckled and shook his head.

"I can promise you, it's real," he assured me, and he squeezed his wife's hand and looked over at her. "Right, Natalie?"

"Of course," Natalie replied, giving me a shy smile. I had met Oliver's wife for the first time earlier this evening, and she seemed very sweet...a little reticent, which surprised me, given how forward Oliver had been from the very first time we had met one another. But then, she spoke French as her first language, and perhaps she was just worried she was going to come out with something that made her sound silly.

We had spent the whole day together. They'd driven me out to the vineyard, shown me the famous grapes that made some of the most expensive bottles in the world (including a few that my brother, Leon, sold as part of his wine company back in New

York). But honestly, there had been pretty much one thing on my mind since we had stepped off the plane, and that was coming to this club Oliver had assured me was the most impressive place in the whole of the city.

"So, you guys have a membership here?" I asked, trying to keep my voice light, not wanting to give away the excitement I was feeling as we approached this famous club. I hadn't been able to find out much about it online. It seemed to me like if you had to ask, you were too lowly to know. I was more than glad I had a couple of people to show me around.

"Yes, we're allowed to bring a guest every time we go," Oliver replied, as he began to slow at the corner of one of the streets. "And it's not like we have many friends interested in this sort of thing, so I suppose it's your lucky night."

"I suppose so," I replied. Honestly, what fascinated me most about this place was how long it seemed to have been going on for. The kink scene in New York was sprawling, but not that deep, with most places usually only lasting a few years before they dropped off again and got replaced by something trendier. But this place had been holding its own in the scene for years now, and I was keen to understand just what it had going for it that was so enduring in the face of so much competition over the years.

We came to a halt outside a heavy red door, and Oliver knocked twice. Someone flicked open a small hatch and peered through to see the two of them standing on the other side.

"*Entrez*," the voice replied curtly, and the door clicked open and the three of us were hustled inside. I grinned. I couldn't believe this was actually happening. See, this was why I loved France so much. Around every corner, it felt like there was history you just couldn't get your hands on back in the States.

As soon as I stepped inside, my eyes widened. Okay, I was

already starting to understand why this place had the reputation that it did. It was stunning. A huge, domed ceiling made room for the dark night sky to pour in through a window at the top, and the place was lit with a deep red, almost hellfire. There were small booths scattered around, as well as a main stage where a couple were already performing a scene. A woman was standing over a man, who was leashed, a collar around his neck and a chain wrapped around her fingers. I only caught a glimpse of them, but the way she was looking at him, it was clear this was far from her first time.

"This way," a hostess greeted us smoothly, but I could hardly pay attention to her as I attempted to take in everything I was seeing around me. This place was...this place was crazy. I liked to think I had seen and experienced a whole lot of what the scene had to offer in the time I had been engaged in it, but it was clear I had only ever scratched the surface. There was a whole lot more for me to uncover before I unwrapped the depths of the desire that were rooted in this place. But I couldn't wait to dig them all up and find out just what they were hiding.

There was a small booth set aside for us, and we slipped into the soft leather seats. Oliver put his arm around Natalie, and I lifted myself up a little so I could get a better look around the place.

"You come here a lot?" I asked them both. Oliver kissed Natalie on the side of her head.

"We do," he replied. "It was Natalie who introduced me to this, actually. She used to work here."

"You used to work here?" I exclaimed with surprise. Of everything I had expected to come out of his mouth, that was about the very bottom of the pile. I couldn't imagine someone like her, someone with her slightly fluttery, nervous attitude, working at a place as devious as this.

"I do have some history, you know," she shot back playfully. If it hadn't been for the husband by her side, I would have thought she was flirting with me, not that I would have minded. But there was so much here for me to take in, I didn't even know where to start. I didn't want to seem too keen, too much of a tourist, but I needed to commit as much of it to memory as I could while I still had the chance. Just had to make sure I didn't let this slip when I was chatting with my family...when they had asked for pictures, I doubted this was the sort of thing they had been imagining.

Before I could get too caught up with peering around, a woman approached the table. She was smiling broadly, her light blonde hair wrapped up into a tight bun on the top of her head.

"Oliver, Natalie, it's lovely to see you," she greeted them both in English, to my surprise. Did she already hear me talking to them? Or maybe they already told her she would be dealing with an American.

"You too, Cecily," Natalie replied, and she rose to her feet and planted a kiss on each of the older woman's cheeks.

"And this must be your guest," she remarked, turning her gaze to me pointedly. Her smile widened a little, tugging at the corners of her face, as though she was having to try her very hardest not to let it split her right open on the spot.

"Yes, I'm Victor," I replied, extending my hand to her. She drew me to my feet at once, planting a kiss on each cheek. The scent of her perfume was a little overwhelming, and I had to bite back the urge to cough in its thick musk.

"Welcome," she murmured to me, looking up at me with a meaningful gaze on her face. "We're so happy to welcome new guests to Petit Mort. I hope you will thoroughly enjoy your stay with us."

"I'm sure I will," I replied. Did she run this place, or something? She must. She was strolling around with such confidence, as though she owned every inch of this room and wanted everyone to know it. It would have been a little funny, if I weren't trying to take everything here seriously right now.

"Have a lovely evening," she remarked, and she drifted off once more. I glanced over at Oliver.

"She's not normally that forward," Oliver remarked, shaking his head. Natalie shrugged. She seemed to be relaxing a little, probably because she was back in a place she knew so well.

"Just glad to have some new guests," she replied, and she caught the eye of a waitress and waved her over.

"*Bonjour*," the waitress greeted us with a warm smile. She was dressed in all black, and it only served to highlight the soft paleness of her skin, the smattering of freckles over her nose. Her red hair was tied back into a loose ponytail, a black velvet bow keeping it back from her face.

"English, please, if you would," Oliver told her gently, nodding to me. "We have a guest."

"Of course," the woman replied, and I was surprised to hear her speak in an American accent. She looked over at me, her green eyes locking on to mine as if she had just been waiting for an excuse to say hello.

"And what can I get for you, sir?" she asked. Just hearing her address me in that way, even though I knew it was simply part of her job, was enough to make me smile. I knew I should have been more careful with the way I let my desire rise when I was here, but this entire place was built around power exchange, around the way we chose to give control or take it from other people. Hard not to hear that word and attach a little more to it than I might have otherwise.

"I'll have a glass of wine," I replied, and she nodded and smiled at me brightly, before checking with Oliver and Natalie that they would just be having their usuals. I let my gaze trail her for a moment as she walked off, the delicious curve of her ass more tempting than it ever should have been.

"Careful, there," Oliver teased me. "I don't think the staff are up for grabs."

"Well, only if you ask nicely," Natalie remarked, squeezing her husband's leg. I could tell they wanted a little privacy, so, as soon as the waitress had returned with my wine, I got to my feet to explore the place a little more.

There were small rooms leading off from the main area. I peered around the doors, but found most of them empty. Ducking in to take a look around, I found most of them were equipped with tools, ties, bindings, impact play stuff, all the things you might need to let someone feel your wrath. Or reward them for taking it so well. I could already feel something stirring inside of me, much as I tried to push it down again. I knew that this wasn't about getting laid, it was just about seeing how things were different over in France. But it was so hard to see all of this, to look at it, and not wish I had someone to share it with...

By the time I emerged once more, the stage that had contained the femdom scene when I had arrived had been switched out for something else. This time, a man was taking the position of power, an older guy standing above a woman who was kneeling at his feet. She was gazing up at him, hands clasped behind her back. He hadn't tied her up or anything, but it was clear he didn't need to. Her submission to him was so complete and so total that it was obvious he could have asked her to do anything he wanted, and she would have jumped at the chance to do anything she could to please him.

He pointed down, to his shoes, and she dropped to all fours at once and began to run her tongue over his loafers as though it was the greatest gift she had ever been given. I felt my cock beginning to ache beneath my pants. I knew I should have contained myself a little better, but it was hard when all I could think about was how much I wished that were me.

I had always been a dominant in the scenes I had played in. Never done anything that intense or that public before, but I had often fantasized about it, about what it would be like to have a woman give her control to me totally. I knew it was the sort of thing you had to do long-term, not just something you could snap your fingers and expect to happen all at once, but I would have given most anything to be able to enjoy that kind of power over someone.

I watched the scene as it unfolded in front of me. The woman, once the man seemed satisfied with everything she had done to clean his shoes, lifted her head and looked at him once more. He reached down, clasped her face in his hand, his fingers digging into her chin, and she didn't take her eyes off him, as though she was waiting for his next order and was so hungry to fulfill it she couldn't contain herself.

He murmured something to her in French, and she slipped her hands back behind her once more. He pulled a rope from his pocket and wrapped it loosely around her wrists, more symbolic than anything else, but strikingly sexy to me. He pushed her down gently, so that her back was arched and her ass was in the air. She was still fully clothed, but it didn't seem to matter. The sight of her like that turned me on so much I could hardly take it. I knew I was going to have to make a concentrated effort to keep my erection from showing. I took another sip of my wine, and averted my eyes from the scene in front of me for a moment and saw that someone else was watching, too.

The waitress. The one with the red hair who had served us before. She was leaning on the wall just outside of the kitchen, and she was gazing up at the scene with the same level of fascination as I was right now. It took her a moment to realize she was being watched, and, a second later, she looked over at me, our eyes locking for a split second. Her cheeks turned bright red, and she glanced away at once, heading back inside the kitchen as though the very last thing on earth that she wanted was to be caught enjoying the show. I smiled, took another sip of my wine. Good to know I wasn't the only one enjoying the art that was taking place in front of me.

The man had a paddle in his hand, wide and thick, and he brought it down with a sharp slap on the rear end of the woman he was playing with. She jumped, and called out. At first, I thought it was just a cry of pain, but then, I realized that was counting in French. *Un.* As he kept hitting her, she kept counting, her voice taking on a wavering edge as he continued, as though she was having a hard time controlling herself and wanting nothing more than for this to end so she could get to whatever it was she was aching for.

He kept hitting her, making her count all the way up to ten, and the sound of her assault echoed through the room. I couldn't take my eyes off her face. The mix of pain and pleasure seemed to have pushed her to some other dimension entirely. I didn't know what was happening to her right now, but she seemed like she didn't want it to end, as though there was something blissful and heavenly about what he was doing to her.

And it was that she enjoyed it so much that turned me on the most. That she seemed unable to contain the pleasure coursing through her in that moment. I kept watching, unable to tear my gaze away, as her face softened and her muscles tensed and everything seemed to focus on nothing more than the shock of how it felt to be hurt by him. This man who seemed to own every inch of her body all at once.

When he was done, there was a silence through the room, and I glanced around once more to see if that waitress might still have been watching. I took another sip of my wine and, before I could so much as register the fact that it was nearly empty, she appeared by my side once more.

"Can I get you another glass, sir?" she asked me. I turned, and smiled when I saw her waiting beside me. Obedient, almost. The look on her face, that eagerness, reminded me of the woman who was on the stage before us.

"That would be wonderful," I replied, and she took the glass from my hands and went to leave, but before she could, I touched her arm, and she stilled on the spot.

"You're American?" I asked her, and she nodded.

"All my life."

"Don't find many of us around here," I remarked, and she laughed.

"I suppose that most of us ending up in a place like this are looking to forget where we came from," she replied.

"You have a point," I agreed, and she paused for a moment.

"What brings you here?" she asked, and she seemed genuinely curious, not just using whatever she could to fill the time and hope for a better tip. I nodded my head in the direction of the stage in front of us, where the man was carefully undoing the ties that had bound his partner and smoothing her hair back from her face gently.

"Curiosity," I replied, and she caught her breath. Had she been thinking about what it might have been like to be up on that stage tonight, too? I wondered if she ever took part in any of the performances. I would have to ask Natalie if that was something they did around here. Because if it was, then I had all the more reason to come back and see her perform.

"I'll get your wine," she murmured, and, with that, she turned and vanished off towards the kitchen once more. I watched as she went, and then returned to the table where Oliver and Natalie were waiting for me.

"Enjoying yourself?" Oliver asked. Natalie's cheeks were

flushed, and I got the feeling the two of them had been sharing a little more than conversation since I had been away. I nodded.

"Oh, I sure am," I replied, and I looked over at the waitress once more and wondered just what it would take to get her in one of those closed-off rooms with me. Because I knew I wasn't going to make it to the end of the night without working out this near-painful tension on someone.

4

LAUREN

THESE NIGHTS WERE ALWAYS THE HARDEST FOR ME.

Not because of the clientele, or anything like that...no, because the performances on the main stage were always so hypnotic. And always filled my head with so many ideas that I didn't even know where to start with beginning to explore them.

Seeing a man take charge of a woman like that, it was something that had always intrigued me. I had been with a few guys who had been into the lighter end of that spectrum of stuff, but every time I watched the pair who came in to perform for our clients, I was reminded just how much more there was of that world for me to find out about.

The thought of it, of giving myself over to someone else for a while...it sounded like damn near the hottest thing in the world for me. I had always been so in control of my own life, and the notion of letting go of that control for a while...there wasn't much better I could imagine if I tried.

But I had never found someone who I would actually have believed it from. That was the problem. All the guys I had been with, both here and back home, had been a little too clean-cut around the edges for me to actually take it seriously when they tried to take control of me. I was always the alpha in the relationship, and I had to hold back giggles when they tried to prove their dominance.

I had tried to distract myself by fussing over the new guest we had in the club tonight. I had never seen him before, and, to my surprise, he was an American. We didn't get many of them around here, given that most Americans would have seen what they got up to in this place as nothing more than some rampant deviance. Even the ones that did come, they tended to be a little more focused on trying to make the point they were so cool and so removed from all of this and that it didn't bother them one little bit, even though it was blatantly obvious when they stared around the place, bug-eyed with surprise at everything that was going on.

But he…he seemed different. There was a twinge of French to his accent, and I wondered if he had spent some time here growing up. Well, not *here* here, at least, I hoped not, but he seemed more comfortable in this place than the few non-Europeans I had laid eyes on.

Or maybe it was just that I thought he was cute. He was there with a couple I had seen a few times before, Oliver and Natalie, and it was clear he wasn't a third to them or anything. He was single, and seemed totally at ease wandering around this place on his own terms, at his own pace. Though he was clearly intrigued by everything he could see going on, he kept his cards close to his chest, and he didn't give too much away.

Though I was sure he had seen me watching the scene that had been playing out on the stage before. And I just had to pray he hadn't noticed the shock of pink to my cheeks as soon as we had locked eyes. Because I had instantly found myself picturing him doing those things to me, and it was going to make getting through the rest of this shift with a straight face way harder than it had to be.

I had been trying to just stay focused on taking care of everything I needed to do right now. There was a lot to think about, keeping this place ticking over, and I didn't want to lose my job just because I had been spending a little too much time focusing on a man who happened to be a little handsome sitting around this place.

More than a little handsome, if I was being honest. With his dark hair that curled down to his neck, his deep brown eyes, and his broad shoulders and strong form, there was something impossibly hot about the way he carried himself. As though he knew he was the most important person in the room, and he didn't care who knew it.

Cecily, the owner of the club, was in today, and I wondered if it had something to do with the American guest that we were hosting this evening. I saw her heading back over to his table a few times, laughing too loudly at the jokes I could hardly make out. She rested a hand on his shoulder a few times, casual but pointed, as though she was making sure anyone watching knew she had first dibs on him.

Cecily never normally made a point to come down here if she could avoid it. It wasn't that she didn't like the place, she assured me, just that she trusted the staff she had appointed to use their discretion to keep things running for her. She was usually off travelling, I heard through the grapevine, exploring the world with the extensive cash she brought in from the memberships to this place. Sounded like a good life, to me.

But she'd had her eye on our new guest the whole night through, and I had to assume there was a reason for that. I managed to catch her as she was coming back into the kitchen to grab a glass of wine.

"Who's the new guy?" I asked her. Cecily traveled enough that I could speak English with her, much to my relief, because my French still wasn't strong enough to play casual about finding out who that slide of sweetness happened to be.

"Oh, him?" she remarked, and she glanced over her shoulder to see if he was looking at her...he wasn't, and a frown crossed her face for an instant before she seemed to brush it off.

"He's a friend of Oliver's," she explained. "They're thinking of going into business together, at least that's what Natalie told me. He's some billionaire, from a rich family in America."

"Damn," I muttered. I couldn't imagine having that kind of money. He could have done anything he wanted in the world with that sort of cash. And yet, here he was, in this club, on this night. Making the effort to talk to me even though I knew he didn't need to.

"Yes, very exciting," she replied, and she patted her hair back into its bun and headed further into the kitchen to get another drink. I knew she must have been beside herself with excitement right now. It wasn't often she even admitted something excited her, but I supposed it was hard to deny when she was clearly so keen on putting the moves on this American.

I still didn't know his name. I was able to glean it from overhearing their conversations...Victor, I was pretty sure...and I brought him his drinks and smiled sweetly every time I came over to join them. It wasn't required of the line of work I was doing, but I made sure that I called him *sir,* too. I liked the look he gave me every time I spoke that word to him, as though he understood just how powerful it was in this setting.

I was pushing the boundaries. Maybe further than I should have. But until he gave me good reason to stop, I didn't see why I should have done so. I was enjoying myself far too much for that, enjoying his attention, the way his gaze lingered on me a little longer than it had to every time I came over. He held his wine well, and, when a new performance started on the stage, the same man and woman from before, after an aftercare break and some rest, he rose to his feet to watch it again.

I couldn't take my eyes off him this time. I knew I shouldn't have been staring so blatantly, but it was hard, when he seemed to draw my eyes everywhere I went. The end of my shift was drawing near, and most of the people who had come to the club that night had begun to file out, but he was there. And he didn't seem intent on going anywhere that he couldn't watch what was happening in front of him right now.

The scene that was playing out was tame, compared to a lot of what I had seen them do before. He was using a cane over her hands, and the sound of the wood against her skin cut through the room with each blow that he rained down on her. I leaned next to the kitchen again, the same place he had caught me watching from, and kept my eyes studiously fixed on the scene in front of me.

But I knew he was watching me.

It almost felt like flirting, what I was doing right now. I knew this was what interested him, and it intrigued me just as much, and the best way I could think of to share that with him was to watch, to let him see I was watching. I cast a glance to him, and his eyes were on me. He moved them away at once, but it was too late, I had seen what he was doing. I smirked to myself. Just the way I wanted it. I could feel a fluttering deep down inside of me, and I did my best to ignore it. I knew I shouldn't have even been entertaining these thoughts right now. But they were way too much fun for me to just ignore them.

I slowly made my way across the room towards him. I could just pretend I was there to serve him, right? To serve him...there was a thought that made my head spin in a way it probably shouldn't have been doing. He watched as I made my way closer to him, and I reached out to take his empty wine glass from him. Our fingers touched for the briefest moment, and I felt a start run down my spine. I tried my best to hide it, though I was sure he would have noticed. In the dark of this room, everything stood out a little more.

Right now, I was off the clock. I shouldn't have been there. I wasn't getting paid for it, and I knew I should have been focusing on getting home, getting some rest for the day at work tomorrow. But I didn't want to. Not when this man was still in the room, not when he seemed so intrigued by the very same things that interested me right now.

"Is there anything else I can help you with?" I asked him, trying to keep my voice as steady as I could manage. He smiled at me.

"What would it take..." he murmured, lowering his voice, shifting a little towards me so he could make sure nobody else in the room was listening to him.

"...to get you into one of those rooms with me?" he finished up, nodding towards the small playrooms that were normally kept locked until one of the paying guests asked for them to be opened. I found myself catching my breath. I didn't know what to say to him right then. I wanted to go with him. I knew those rooms like the back of my hand, but there was something to be said for a little restraint. If I got caught fooling around with one of the guests...well, I had no idea what the rules were about that, but I doubted they would be looked on too fondly. Especially not when my boss clearly had more than a hint of interest in him.

But I couldn't ignore the throbbing between my thighs. The thrill of his attention on me. This man could have had anyone in this city that he looked at twice, but he wanted me. And he wanted me, I was sure, in the same way that that man had wanted the woman he had performed with tonight.

"Let me see if they're open for you," I whispered back, still playing, for at least a little longer, at being the gracious, helpful hostess. He didn't know I was off the clock, after all. I could still play this off as just making sure this was all about taking care of his needs. Not...well, taking care of the other needs that might have been pressing urgently on him right now.

I moved towards the playrooms, trying to ignore the way my head was spinning with excitement at the thought of everything I wanted to do to him. I knew I needed to have him. It was the first time I had felt that kind of attraction to anyone in so long that I could hardly remember what it felt like. Yes, I found myself aroused by the performances sometimes, but never feeling the need to take it out on anyone. But with him? With him, it was different.

What would he think of me? My mind was racing. I didn't want him assuming I was some sort of prostitute, there for the taking. But I couldn't stop this now. I didn't want to. I needed to feel him, to see how far he would take this...to find out just how much experience he had with all of this and what he could show me of this world that had intrigued me for such a long time now.

The playroom was unlocked, and I stepped inside, reaching for the light. As soon as it was on, it cast the room into a soft pink glow, that seemed made for romance. Or something more. And I had hardly had time to turn around before I felt his hands on my waist, pulling me close to him, and I knew there was nothing that could convince me of just how bad an idea this happened to be.

I didn't care. I just wanted him. I turned to face him, wrapping my arms tight around him and kissing him as his lips found mine. The taste of him was intoxicating...wine, musk, something smoky that filled my lungs and told me this was dangerous, but I didn't care.

"Limits?" he asked me, sliding his hands down to sink into my ass. "Safe word?"

"What do you..." I blurted out, before I realized what he was talking about. Honestly, I didn't have time to think about all that right now. I just needed him to fuck me. Everything else could wait. I fully intended on getting there soon, but for this moment, all that my body needed was the raw, primal feeling of him deep inside of me.

"Just fuck me," I pleaded with him, and I reached for the condoms where I knew they were kept in a small drawer next to the door. I had filled up this very container just a few days before, not knowing for a second I would be the one using them next. I pushed one into his hand, and he turned me around, pressed me forcefully against the door as his hands roamed down, under my shirt, pushing it up so he could grasp my bare breasts beneath the fabric.

"Fuck," he growled into my ear, letting the word slither into my brain and making me shiver. I hardly knew this man's name, but it didn't matter. I didn't need to. All that mattered was the way his body felt against mine, the chemistry that burned between us as soon as he touched me. He rolled up my skirt and sank his fingers roughly into my ass, and I tipped my head back against his shoulder and let out a moan. If anyone I worked with right now was to walk in on the two of us together, I knew they would never look at me in the same way again, but frankly, I didn't care one little bit. I wanted to get fucked right now. I had waited long enough to feel something like this, and now I had found the person who turned on that desire within me, there was nothing on earth that could get me to stop.

He ripped my panties down and tore open the condom with his teeth. I could already feel my urgent wetness sliding down the inside of my thighs, and I realized I had been waiting too long for this, all night long to the point that I couldn't wait any longer. I arched my back, pushed myself towards him, telling him every way I knew how, that I needed him and I wanted to feel him deep inside of me.

And he didn't make me wait long. He rolled the condom on, and planted his cock at the entrance of my pussy, holding it there for a moment.

"You ready?" he murmured, and I nodded.

"Please," I whined, my voice edged with a desperation I had never had in it before. Slowly, he pushed himself inside of me, taking his time, making sure I could feel every inch of him as he slid all the way inside my pussy.

The fullness was almost more than I could take. His cock was thick, spreading me wide around him so I could fit every inch of him inside of me. I groaned and tried to sink my hands into the wood in front of me, needing more, needing every second of this. He grasped my hips and pulled me back against him roughly, thrusting all the way up to the hilt and making me shiver helplessly.

"Tell me how it feels," he demanded, sliding his hand up my neck and grasping my face, just like the guy had done on the stage not long before.

"It feels...big," I groaned. I couldn't exactly get into heavy descriptors right now. My brain didn't work...didn't want to, right in that instant.

"Good," he murmured, and he pushed a little deeper inside of me, holding himself there, letting me get used to the invasion of my pussy as he took me without holding back. Grinding his hips against me, he hit every inch of me from the inside out, one hand still on my hip, and I groaned once more. This time, he slipped his fingers into my mouth to keep me quiet, and I obediently parted my lips and rolled my tongue around the taste of him.

"Good girl," he told me. I wanted to hear him call me that again and again and again. The rush of knowing I was doing everything right, that I was giving him everything he wanted from me, made my brain feel like it was tingling from the inside out. If there was anything sweeter than this, I had yet to feel it.

He started moving harder then, thrusting into me roughly, spreading me around him and holding me steady as he used my body to take everything he wanted from me. And I gave in, totally. I had no recourse now. I just wanted him to take me like this, to use me any way he wanted me to, and it was enough to make my brain feel like it was switching off, turning on to something else entirely. And I liked it. I knew this must have been what those girls felt when they were up on the platforms, trying to control themselves as the men who owned them showed them just what they thought of them. And I was starting to see, clearer than ever, just why that was as impossibly erotic as it seemed.

It didn't take long until I felt a burning desire begin to rise up and take control of me. How could it not? The pressure between my legs made my heart feel like it was going to come bursting right out of my chest, and I just had to grip tight to the wall to keep myself from collapsing to the ground entirely. But he kept moving inside of me, kept pistoning that perfect dick into my pussy over and over again, relentless, unable to let me off for a second.

When I came, I cried out, my body trembling and then crumpling for a moment as I tried to make sense of what was going through my mind. I had never given myself to anyone like this before, let them own me in this way, but I knew, in the very instant that I felt him finish too, it was everything I had needed. My knees were shaking and my vision was blurry around the edges, and I didn't even really know who this man was, but I wished I could have felt him empty his seed inside of me with nothing to hold us back. I wished I could have focused on the delicious sensation of his release as he finished deep within me.

He wrapped his arms around me, planted a kiss against the

back of my neck, and I sighed with pleasure and let myself slowly, slowly drift back down to earth. The sensation was...well, it was one thing, that was for sure. But it was the power he had taken from me that really served to push this into another dimension. I'd been with men before, been with men who fucked me well, but nothing like this. Nothing that made me feel the way he did right now.

He held himself inside of me for a long moment, as though he was reluctant to pull himself loose when he had been enjoying himself so damn much. But, finally, eventually, he did, and he turned me around so I was facing him again and pushed me back against the wall, his tongue in my mouth, his teeth catching on my lip and making my toes curl helplessly in my shoes.

When he pulled back, I looked into his eyes and tried to find something inside of me to tell him everything I was feeling right now. But I came up with a dead blank. All I could do was stare at him, open-mouthed, agape, like I had never felt anything like that before in my life.

And there was only one question on my mind...and that was just how long he was going to be staying in town. Because there was no way in hell I was going to let a man like that slip through my fingers before I was done with him. He seemed to be reading my mind, and he just kissed me again, sliding his hands down my body so he could push my panties back up my legs once more. I had no idea what the hell had just happened, but I knew for certain I had enjoyed every single moment of it. And I knew I was going to have to indulge it again sometime soon. And I couldn't wait.

5

VICTOR

I CAME TO THE NEXT MORNING WITH A SMILE ON MY FACE. Though it took a moment for me to remember just what it was that had put it there.

But then, it all came flooding back to me...at the club last night, that girl who had been working there. Slipping into one of the rooms while her boss had had her back turned. And pulling down her panties and pushing myself inside of her and fucking her furiously while she clung to the wall for dear life.

Yeah. That was a pretty good reason to wake up with a smile on your face, right?

I peeled myself out of bed and headed to the shower. I had no idea how I had made it home last night. I hadn't been drunk or anything, but the passion of what I had shared with that woman had been enough to turn the rest of my memories into mush. All I could think about was her, her, her, and just how long it would take before I got to see her again.

She was an American, too. I wondered how long she had been out here in France, how many years she had spent in this place, and how long she intended to stay. She seemed confident in the way she moved in that place, as though she was certain she had long since earned her place there and nobody was going to be able to take that away from her. I couldn't see how anyone would ever dare.

I had stuff to do that morning, a meeting with Oliver down at the vineyard so we could start going over some of the details of this deal I wanted to pull together with him. And I knew that was why I had come here in the first place, but, truth be told, I was only able to think about one thing and one thing alone as I stood there under the cool rush of the shower, and that was the woman who I had been with last night.

I couldn't help but wonder if she had been part of the scene for a long time. She must have known it pretty well from working at a place like that, even if she wasn't a part of it herself. She seemed to understand the dynamic well, well enough that when I moved to take control she was quick to let it happen. Had she got other partners? Most people who engaged with a scene like that one rarely stuck to just one partner at a time, but I had to admit the thought of her with someone else sent a flare of possessiveness up my spine. I knew I had no right to be feeling that way about her, but I couldn't help it. It had been a long time since I had felt that surge of need for someone, and known they felt the very same thing right in return, but I didn't want to give it up now I had it.

Or now I thought I did, anyway. I climbed out of the shower and threw on some clothes, heading downstairs to meet the car Oliver had told me he would send for me as soon as he got the chance. I wondered if he and Natalie had had as good a night as I had or if they had somehow found out about the little liaison I'd had with the woman who was meant to be serving us all night long.

It was a natural shift, really, from serving to service like that. I loved the idea of it, of her carefully and pointedly taking care of everything we needed from her all evening long, and then sliding into another form of it as soon as we were alone together. How long had she been looking at me through that night and wondering what it might have been like to have me take control of her? The thought was intoxicating, enervating, and I wished I could go to her again and tell her I wasn't going to be able to get her out of my head anytime soon.

Maybe she had wound up in trouble for what she had done. After all, I doubted it was exactly normal for a guest to slide into bed with a customer...not bed, exactly, but in the metaphorical sense. Up against the wall had always been way much more fun to me, anyway.

I had to push those thoughts to the back of my mind as I greeted the driver and he took me across the city and towards the outskirts, where Natalie and Oliver ran their business. I wondered, for a moment, just how they had discovered their own dynamic together; it was clear the two of them loved each other's company and enjoyed nothing more than slipping out of their marital bliss into something a little kinkier. But they had made it work long-term. Perhaps there was something to be said for all of it, for indulging a darker side to your life, even when you were meant to be playing at the goody-two-shoes married couple.

I had never really considered, honestly, that kink would be anything other than a supplement to the life that I already led. Nothing that could be centered in the way I existed, in how I chose to live. But some part of me, something deep down inside of me, was intrigued by the idea, and I knew I was going to have to get a couple of drinks in Oliver so I could ask him outright about the nature of his dynamic with his wife and just how he kept it fresh after all those years.

It was starting to rain slightly by the time I arrived at the vineyard, but I didn't mind...in fact, the light mist and soft drizzle made the whole place look as though it could have come straight from a picture book. I stepped out of the car and Natalie hurried over from the main building to greet me, her coat pulled up over her head so she could ward off the worst of the rain.

"Good to see you," she greeted me with a smile. She seemed a little more confident than she had the day before, and I wondered if she simply struggled a little with new people. Or perhaps she felt as if, now that she had allowed me to see just how adventurous her sex life could be, she had nothing to hide any longer.

"You too," I replied. "I'm so looking forward to seeing everything about the way you run this place..."

"*Alors,* we want you to have a good idea of what you're investing in," she pointed out, as she stepped through the door of the main building and brushed a few drops off her coat. "So, this is where we start with the business side of things..."

I followed her through the office, where she showed me the way they ran things. They were connected with a number of wine suppliers, who came to them every year for their harvest. I knew plenty about the industry already, but I listened to her patiently, wanting to show them I was totally engaged with the thought of everything that came next. I needed them to believe I was the perfect choice for this investment, and I knew that flattering their egos for the way they ran things was the best way to do it.

I had to admit, though, I started to perk up a little bit once they suggested I do a little tasting of some of their in-house brand for that year; I was more than happy to share my take on it, and Oliver, just back from a loop around the yard, poured me a generous glass and handed it over. As soon as his wife was out of earshot, he turned to me with his eyebrows raised.

"So, how did you enjoy last night?" he asked me with enthusiasm. I nodded.

"It was a lot of fun," I admitted. He grinned.

"I saw you were talking to the waitress a lot," he pointed out. "Something going on there?"

My mind flashed back to everything that had happened the night before. I wasn't sure I was ready to actually talk to him about any of it, at least right now. There was too much going on inside my head for the time being, and I didn't want to spill anything more than I needed to. Things might have been fun, but I didn't want to assume anything else was going to come of them when I really didn't know this girl at all. I might have liked her, liked what we shared together, but that was where it ended. I shrugged.

"I don't think so," I lied quickly. "But I wouldn't mind going back sometime soon, if you don't mind abusing your guest pass to get me in...?"

"Hey, I didn't bring you all the way out here just for the business," he joked, slapping a hand on to my shoulder. "I'd love to. Just let me know when works for you and we'll get you out there again..."

He trailed off just as his wife entered the room once more, and winked at me to let me know we would pick up on this later. I grinned back at him. I knew coming here had been the right choice for me. Life in New York, while it might have been closer to my family, was starting to get a little old. And I knew there was far too much out here in the rest of the world for me to explore to ever feel happy hiding out back there.

6

LAUREN

I hustled to get my ass ready for work, keeping an eye on the time as I went, and trying to ignore the soreness between my legs that offered a delicious reminder of everything that had happened the night before.

I still couldn't quite believe I had really done it. I knew it was totally crazy, and if I got caught in the act of giving myself to a guest there would no doubt be hell to pay. But I didn't care. How could I, when everything just felt like it was meant to be? The tension between us all night long, the way he laid hands on me as though he wanted me to know that he owned me. God, there was nothing better than that. I was never going to be able to recover from how intense it had been and how much I wanted to repeat it, over and over again…

But I was going to have to. I didn't even know if the dude was going to come back to the club again. He was an American, and he might have only been in town for a matter of days. Which would leave me with nothing more than the memory of everything we had shared, and the craving to find someone who could do that all again. Who could make me feel the way that he could.

I had pulled a shift at the bakery that morning, and one of the girls I worked with, Elodie, had noticed there was something different about me. She didn't know I worked at the Petit Mort, and I wanted to keep it that way for as long as I could, but I supposed the smirk on my face was hard for her to ignore.

"Did something happen last night?" she asked me, and I shook my head at once.

"No, just a long night," I replied, feigning a yawn. It was true, but I wasn't tired. I felt as though I had been jolted full of electricity, like I could have run up a mountain before lunchtime. She eyed me for a moment, clearly not buying it.

"*Bien*," she replied, but I knew she was keen to try and get more out of me. Out of everyone I had met in this town, she was about the biggest gossip out of the lot of them, and I knew she would be trying to tease the story of what had really happened out of me for the next three weeks if she had to.

But now I was heading back to the club, and I couldn't stop wondering if he was going to be there. I hoped so. The thought of it, of his hands on me again, of his eyes meeting mine and sharing the carnal knowledge of everything we had done together...it was already exciting to me. And I couldn't wait to see just how much of these fantasies of mine were going to wind up coming true.

But when I got to work, there was someone waiting for me, and about the last someone, actually, that I hoped to be intercepted by when I walked through the door. With her arms crossed over her chest, Cecily waylaid me before I could get to the kitchen.

"I need to talk to you," she told me, and I nodded at once. I had seen her in this mood a few times before, and I knew there was no point on earth in arguing with her.

"What's wrong?" I asked her, as sweetly as I could. I knew there were no cameras in the playrooms, so there was no way she could have seen what I had done in there the other day with that man, but I wouldn't have been surprised if someone had spilled the beans on me anyway. I hadn't exactly been subtle, emerging from there probably looking as though I had been pulled through a hedge backwards, cheeks flushed and smiling wide as I guided him back into the club once more.

"That man who was here the other night," she began. I cocked my head to the side, feigning ignorance.

"Which man?" I asked her. She glared at me for a moment, and I fought the urge to wither into myself. I knew this was how she had stayed on top for as long as she had, how she commanded the respect that she did. She didn't take shit, and she didn't allow anyone to treat her like a fool. But I hoped she would let me get away with it. Just this one time. Because the very last thing I needed right now was for her to figure out everything I had been trying to hide.

"The American," she continued, her voice calm and composed, like she was daring me to continue to try and string her along like this. "The one you were serving."

"I remember him," I replied, finally, figuring there was no point trying to brush this off any longer.

"I'm sure you do," she replied, voice icy-cold. "I want you to know he'll be coming back here tomorrow night. His hosts have tapped him as their guest once again."

"Oh, and you want me to serve him again."

"I want to make sure you're keeping your focus on your job," she replied. I knew what she was trying to tell me, even if she wasn't going to come right out and say it. I couldn't blame her. I tried to ignore the heat sliding up my cheeks, tried to ignore the way it was giving me away right now. I had to stay cool. I had to make sure I didn't let her get under my skin. She couldn't prove anything. I could just say I had dropped a glass of wine on myself and that's why I looked so flushed and askew when we had come out of that room. Even if she knew it was a lie, she knew she couldn't fire me over something she would never prove.

"Of course I am," I replied carefully. "You know how much I value my position here, Cecily. I wouldn't do anything to put that in danger."

"I'm glad to hear it."

Her voice was clipped, and I knew she was telling me in no uncertain terms just what she thought of me. She must have known what had happened between me and that man, and she intended to make sure it never went down like that again. Or I never went down on him again. Or something.

"Thank you for your time," she told me, and, with that, she turned on her heel and marched off into the club once more, and I found myself wondering just how serious she was about that order. And just why she might have been so committed to the idea of making sure this man didn't get anywhere close to me. I was curious, no denying it, about the way she felt about him, but she was my boss, and asking any more questions would only serve to drag more out of this already-dangerous situation. I had to stay focused on what mattered, and that was making sure I did everything I could to keep hold of this job.

Even if that meant going out of my way to avoid running into the man I couldn't get out of my head. And hope he didn't do anything to tempt me beyond the point that I could take it, either.

7

VICTOR

As soon as I stepped into the club once more, I felt as though a weight had been lifted from my shoulders. I grinned as I moved through it, unable to keep the smile off my face. God, it felt good to be back here.

I scanned the room at once, searching for Lauren, the woman I had been with the other night. I had no idea if she was working again, but I could just sense her presence here somewhere, even if I couldn't quite place it yet. I knew I would find her again. I knew we would find one another again. And I knew it was going to be everything I needed to blow off the steam of the tension that had been building inside of me all day long.

We had been down at the vineyard all day, and I had started to get bored by lunchtime. Not that I thought this was anything other than a great deal, of course. I still wanted to work with Natalie and Oliver, and I knew they were the best bet I had to find a business in France that matched with everything I was interested in. But I was starting to get restless, thinking about coming back to this place, and I knew it was starting to grow, already, into an addiction I might not have entire control of.

But that was how it had been when all of this had started, too. When I had discovered this world, I had wanted to indulge myself in it every single way I could. How could I not? I had waited so long to uncover the truth of the way I felt about all of this, and as soon as I did, it seemed like it would have been just rude not to do something worthwhile with it.

And that woman, the woman who had been here last time, she had sent a fireball through my system. I knew I had to have her again. I wasn't going to be satisfied until I got my hands on her once more. So, now...where the hell was she?

We were led to our table, and Cecily, the owner, came to join us once more. This time, though, she wasn't just settling on checking we were doing okay. She came right down and sat next to us, much to my surprise. That was the last thing I had been expecting from her. I mean, yes, I knew she owned the place, but that didn't mean she had to come out swinging, right? I was distracted, scanning the room for Lauren, and unable to find her.

"It's wonderful to see you back again so soon, Victor," she told me, reaching over to touch my arm lightly. Even with the warm smile on her face and the suggestive edge to her voice, I couldn't stay focused on the woman in front of me.

"Yes, I'm glad to be back," I replied, and I glanced around the room some more. My eyes flicked over the scene on the stage, something focused on ropes and bindings, something I might have been fascinated by if it hadn't been for the fact that I couldn't stop thinking about the woman I knew was here somewhere.

"If there's anything at all I can do to make your time here with us more comfortable," she murmured, leaning forward a little and flicking her tongue over her red-lacquered lips... It was clear she was addressing this part of the conversation to me and to me alone, judging by how ignorant she seemed of Oliver and Natalie's presence right there at the table with us.

"You'll be sure to let me know, won't you?" she asked. I nodded.

"Of course," I replied. But I got the feeling that if I had been honest with her, and told her all I could think about right now was getting my hands on the woman I had seen last time, she would have been less than impressed.

She smiled at me once more and rose to her feet to leave us alone again, and, as soon as she was gone, Natalie let out a giggle of surprise.

"I don't think I've ever seen her like that before," she remarked. I looked over at her.

"Like what?"

"Like...that!" She laughed. "She was coming on to you like crazy."

"Yeah, she really was," Oliver agreed, as he draped an arm around his wife casually. It was almost as though seeing another woman attracted to me had been enough to make him worry his own might suddenly let her eye wander. I almost wanted to remind him that Natalie had never so much as looked at me twice when he wasn't around, but that might have been presumptive.

"Do you think she's into you?" Natalie asked, her eyes widening as she leaned towards me with interest.

"I guess she might be," I agreed. I was still distracted, didn't care much whether she was into me or not. I just wanted to find Lauren again. I knew she must have been here. It was almost as though I could sense her somewhere, though I was sure that was ridiculous. It was just hard to deny the truth of the temptation I felt when I was in this place again, this sureness that this was going to go the way I wanted it to...

And that was when I spotted her.

She was serving another table, bringing out their wine and placing it down carefully in front of them. They barely paid attention to her, too caught up in the conversation they were already having, but I couldn't take my eyes off of her. It was almost surreal, seeing her in person again, and the temptation was already burning deep inside of me. I needed this. Needed her. And, before I could stop myself, I made my excuses to Natalie and Oliver and rose to my feet again.

I managed to intercept her before she reached the kitchen once more. She paused and looked up at me, clearly a little nervous about being so close to me again.

"Hey," I greeted her. It didn't feel like enough to put across everything I had been thinking about, everything I had been feeling since the last time I'd seen her, but I had to start somewhere, didn't I? This was as good a place as any...

"Can I help you with anything?" she asked me, her voice careful, as though she didn't want to let something slip that she should have been keeping to herself. I shook my head.

"I was hoping you might be able to show me a little more of those playrooms," I told her, lowering my voice and letting a smile flick up my lips. A small smirk crossed over her mouth before she could stop it. Though she might have been trying to play at professional, I knew she had enjoyed what we'd done as much as I had, and that it was as impossible for her to deny that chemistry as it was for me.

"I'd be happy to get one of my colleagues to show you around," she replied. I stared at her for a moment, trying to work out what had changed, trying to work out what had shifted.

"Did I do something wrong?" I asked her, and she shook her head at once...and then, shooting a quick look around us to make sure we weren't being listened to, she lowered her voice and explained.

"I think someone must have seen us together before," she

admitted. "When we were...in the playroom. I'm not meant to get so close to customers. My boss told me I wasn't to get too close to you again, and I don't want to lose this job."

"Is that what you want?" I asked her. "For me to stay away from you?"

She chewed her lip and looked up at me, and then shook her head.

"No," she confessed, and her voice was edged with desire. "No, it's not."

"Then don't," I murmured to her, and I pulled the card of the hotel I was staying at from my pocket. "Here. Take this. If you want to come by later...just ask for me. Victor Rousso. They'll give you my room number. I'll be waiting."

I pushed the card into her hand and she looked down at it for a moment like she wasn't sure she should really be holding this. But then, seemingly before she could talk herself out of it, she tucked it into the pocket of her apron and flashed me a smile.

"I guess I might see you later, then," she replied. I grinned at her.

"I guess you might," I replied. But then, her eyes slipped behind me, and she seemed to notice someone looking at us. She quickly pushed open the kitchen door and hurried inside, leaving me with nothing more than the sweet scent of her hair and the urge to kiss her again.

But she had my card. That counted for something. And I would wait out the rest of the night to find out just what that was if I had to.

I returned to the table once more and sipped on my drink as I watched the rope performance in front of me. It was amazing how they could get their bodies to twist and turn in such a way, how the delicate ropes could form into such unyielding knots around the bodies of the people that they were trapping. And I couldn't help but wonder, as I took it all in, just what Lauren might have made of being trussed up like that. Totally helpless...

"Something on your mind?" Oliver asked me. Natalie had gone to chat with a few of her old friends whom she had worked with at this place, leaving Oliver and me alone once more. I shook my head.

"Just enjoying the show," I replied, gesturing to the performance in front of us. In truth, though, my mind was starting to wander a little...specifically, to wander to Cecily, and just what her intentions had been when she had come over here to try to chat me up.

Because she must have been the one who had told Lauren to stay away from me. I doubted she knew for sure what we had done, but she likely had some vague idea of what we'd been getting up to. Perhaps that is what had thrown her so badly, what had made her so irritated as to ask Lauren to stay away from me.

Did she want me for herself? Maybe. Natalie seemed certain she had been flirting with me before, and it wouldn't have surprised me. My family name travelled a long way ahead of me these days, whether I liked it or not, and I knew that being a Rousso would be enough for certain women to set their sights on you.

But I had no interest in her at all. She seemed perfectly pleasant, but there was something about Lauren, about the way the two of us had felt that impossible-to-deny connection between us. There was no way anyone could have ignored it. I knew I had to have her again, and I knew she felt just the same way I did. The connection between us, whatever it was, was far too much for me to deny, and there was no way in hell I was going to skip out on getting to feel it again.

I caught her eye a few times over the course of the evening, and, each time I did, I could have sworn I saw her cheeks flush a deeper shade of red. Just the way I liked it. I wanted her to be ready for me, keen for me, needy for me. Ready to do anything at all on earth I asked her to by the time I got her alone again. And I got the feeling I was going to be gifted exactly that.

The rest of the evening past by at a comfortable pace. Natalie brought a few of her friends back to the table so I could meet them, excitedly introducing me, and the conversation flowed easily, even as the performers were taking things to the next level between us. As I tried to stay focused on the people in front of me, I couldn't help but feel that tense push of awareness... knowing where she was, every time she moved, who she was talking to and what she was doing. A couple of times, Lauren actually came over to the table to serve us, and our eyes locked for an instant as though we were sharing some secret we didn't want to speak out loud.

At least, not yet.

I tried to keep my head in the game, but by the time we were ready to go, I was practically itching to get out of there. Lauren seemed to have vanished a little while before, presumably at the end of her shift, and I intended to do everything I could to meet her back at the hotel the way I had promised I would.

I strode out into the dark of the Brittany night by myself, promising Oliver and Natalie I was happy to walk home alone. It had started to rain again by the time I stepped out of the club, but the soft drizzle was enough to take the edge off the desire that seemed to be burning me up from the inside out. I couldn't wait for her a moment longer. I traversed the quiet streets and counted the steps until I could get to see her again, prayed she was going to have taken me up and was waiting for me right now outside the hotel.

And, when I turned the corner and found her standing

there, I grinned. Because I knew she was as hungry for me as I was for her. I closed the gap between us, pushed a strand of drenched hair back from her face, and kissed her hard, pushing my tongue into her mouth, and sinking my body against hers like this was what I had been waiting for from the moment I had stepped out the door.

8

LAUREN

I wasn't sure exactly how we managed to make it up to his room. From the moment his mouth met mine, I hadn't been able to think straight. The only thing I had been able to focus on was the way he tasted, of wine and rain and desire, and just how much trouble I was going to get in if my boss found out I was doing something as naughty as this.

But I didn't care. I had to pleasure him once more. I had to do everything I could to prove to him this was real, that the desire and the intensity that had been there between us before wasn't a fluke. As soon as I had seen him at the club earlier tonight, I had known there was no way I was going to be able to handle sticking to the rules Cecily had laid out for me. Not when he looked that good. Not when I knew just how he could make me feel.

But she couldn't tell me what I could do when I was outside of work, could she? And, as we tumbled over the threshold of his room together, I promised myself I wasn't going to make a habit of defying my boss, not when I knew she was the one who was responsible for paying my bills. But when he laid it out for me like this, too tempting to deny...how the hell could I tell him no?

"You have no idea how much I wanted you tonight," he growled into my ear, as he reached down and grasped hold of my ass to push me against his hardened cock. I felt my knees starting to shake. I had to have him. But more than that...I had to show him how much I wanted him.

"Can you show me?" I breathed to him. I didn't know exactly how he was going to react to that statement, but I wanted him to take control again. I didn't know how to tell him exactly what I desired, but I knew I wasn't going to be satisfied until I felt him take that power from me again, until I felt him take the control I knew he wanted.

"How far are you willing to go?" he murmured back, catching my earlobe in his mouth and sinking his teeth into it for a moment. I shivered.

"As far as you want," I replied. And, with that, he planted his hand on my shoulder, and pushed me down to my knees in front of him.

I gazed up at him, my heart pounding hard in my chest. I couldn't think about anything but how intense my desire was to serve him in that moment. And I knew it was crazy, I knew I shouldn't have been so aroused by this, but how could I not be? As he slowly reached down to cup my head in his hand, tilting my chin up towards him, I parted my lips at once, and he pushed his thumb into my mouth so I could taste him. I sucked softly, knowing it was going to be replaced with something a hell of a lot more delicious soon.

"Good girl," he told me, and I felt a shiver of delight when I heard him call me that. I knew I would never get tired of knowing I was pleasing him.

He reached down to unzip his pants, taking his time and guiding his erection into his hand. He was already fully hard, and the sight of him close-up like this was enough to make my stomach tingle. He was thicker than I thought, his cock so tempting I actually licked my lips as soon as I saw it.

"Show me how good you are," he ordered me, voice low, leaving no room for argument. And, not taking my eyes off him, I parted my lips, leaned forward, and did just that.

I could taste the drop of precum on his tip, the salty sweetness filling my mouth and coating my tongue. I let out a soft moan, and he pushed his hips a little forward, thrusting into my mouth. The thought of him using me like this, taking me just the way he wanted to, was impossibly sexy to me, and I found myself reaching up and sinking my fingers into his thighs, pulling him further into me. God, he tasted so good…the velvety smoothness of his erection was delicious, and I swirled my tongue against his shaft.

He let out a low groan, and I sealed my lips around him and slid my mouth up and down his full length. I had never been the biggest fan of giving oral sex, but there was something about this right now that was changing my mind completely. Something about the way he tasted, about the way it made me feel…about how it felt to lavish his cock with attention, to show him that I was willing to do anything at all to please him.

I flicked my gaze up to meet him as he began to slide himself back into me, meeting the movement of my mouth with his hips. I felt his thick tip hit the back of my throat, and, to my surprise, instead of having to catch my breath it just slipped down my mouth, and I found myself taking every inch of him at once. My nose was buried against his pubic hair, and I closed my eyes and focused on the warmth of the sensation of his length down my throat.

"Look at me," he ordered me, and I looked up, meeting his gaze as best I could. My eyes were starting to water, but I didn't care. I just wanted to show him how much I wanted him. How much I desired him. And how much, above all of it, I needed him right now. Needed him to take control from me.

He cupped my chin in his hand again and used the leverage to fuck my mouth mercilessly. I was stunned at how easy it was for me to take his full length down my throat, but I didn't break his gaze for a moment. I needed to show him how good I was at this. How good I was for him. I grasped tightly to his thighs, pulling him into me, greedy for everything that he could give me...greedy for everything I could take from him. He groaned, his hand moving to my hair, balling in it roughly to keep me in place as he used my mouth to get him where he needed to go.

And it didn't take long until I felt his cock starting to swell in my throat. He paused for a moment, held himself deep inside of me, and looked down at me, his eyes burning with lust and want. And I knew I was giving him everything he had wanted from me. I felt a flood of desire between my legs, and he suddenly pulled back from me so I could catch my breath.

"Open your mouth," he ordered, and I parted my lips at once and extended my tongue, letting him know I was willing to take anything he wanted to give me. He stroked his cock once, twice, and then came over my lips and my tongue. The taste of his seed intensified the desire burning between my legs, and I knew I was already addicted to the way it made me feel.

I leaned forward and swirled my tongue around his tip, cleaning up the last of him before he tucked himself away once more. And I knew whatever was going to happen for the rest of tonight, we had just confirmed that this was more than a one-time thing. That we were more than just a one-off fling.

And I couldn't wait to see just what else he had in store for me. As he pulled me to my feet and tossed me back on the bed behind him, I was sure this was going to be the best-spent night I'd had in a hell of a long time. And I intended to make the very most of it that I possibly could.

9

VICTOR

When I woke up the next morning, and reached over to the other side of the bed, I knew she was going to be there.

And that was the best feeling in the world.

Next to me lay the sleeping body of the woman I had spent the night with. Lauren and I, once we had come home from the club, had passed the next few hours completely selfishly, enjoying every inch of each other we could, as she let me take control of her body totally and allowed me to do anything I wanted to please myself with her.

By the time we had both climaxed more times than we could count, we fell into bed together and she slept with her head resting on my chest. It wasn't what I expected, not really, but as long as her boss was going to make it impossible for me to actually have so much as a conversation with her while she was at the club, I didn't see what other choices I had.

I pulled her against me, running my hand down the curve of her waist and feeling the tempting arch of her body even as she dozed and tried to recoup some of the energy we had spent together the night before. Nuzzling my face against her hair, I inhaled her smell, closed my eyes, and let myself get lost in it. If there was much better than this, right here, then I had yet to find it.

I knew I wasn't going to be able to get her out of my head that easily. I had wondered if we both just needed to work out some desire on each other for the time being, but clearly, this went further than that. Sex would have been one thing, but this was about power, control, the addictive rush of handing it to someone else. I knew we had found something solid, something we weren't going to be able to shake free of anytime soon.

And, as she stirred in my arms, I planted a kiss on the back of her neck and let my hand slide down the front of her body. She squirmed against me happily and half-turned her head so she could look at me.

"Well, good morning," she murmured, and I brushed my lips across her cheek.

"Good morning," I replied. "You sleep well?"

"Hmm, could have been better," she admitted, turning to face me with a smile on her face. "I had this guy keeping me up all night long."

"You'll have to tell me who he is," I murmured back, "so I can take care of him."

"Oh, I don't think he needs anything like that," she smirked playfully, and she wrapped her arms around me and snuggled against me...and then, all at once, she froze.

"What is it?" I asked her, pulling back and seeing the look of horror on her face. Her eyes were pinned to the clock on the bedside table, and it looked as though all the blood had gone rushing right out of her face there and then.

"I need to get to work!" she exclaimed, and she bounded out of bed and started grabbing her clothes as hastily as she could.

"I thought the club didn't open until later," I pointed out, a little confused, but she shook her head.

"It's not the work at the club," she explained. "I have another job, too. As a pastry chef. And if I'm not there in the next twenty minutes, they're going to fire me on the spot."

"Shit," I replied, and I couldn't help but chuckle at how dramatic she was being as she fumbled with her shirt and pulled her hair back hurriedly. Plus, it was kind of distracting to see the delicious curve of her body walking around this bedroom and to know I wasn't meant to do anything about it. How was I meant to just pretend I didn't see how hot she was?

"You need a ride down there?" I asked her, and she shook her head.

"It's just around the corner," she replied. "I can walk it."

"Well, then, let me walk you there," I suggested, and she paused for a moment, seemingly surprised by my offer.

"You mean it?" she asked, and I nodded.

"Of course I do," I replied. "Come on, I don't want you to be late."

I threw on some clothes, and, before I knew it, the two of us were out on the street, enjoying the clear, cold morning air. She kept checking her watch, but eventually, she let out a breath of relief and shook her head.

"Okay, I think I'm going to make it there in time," she explained. "I'll live to fight another day."

"Or bake," I suggested. "I didn't take you for a baker, I have to admit."

"Well, what did you take me for?" she wondered aloud with curiosity.

"I suppose when you meet someone in a kink club, it's hard to think of them doing something so...mainstream," I explained. She laughed.

"And I guess you can't get much more mainstream in France than baking," she mused out loud.

"How long have you been doing that? The baking, I mean?" I asked her.

"Well, I studied it back in America," she replied. "But I decided I wanted to come here and do something a little more exciting than just making bagels in New York, you know?"

"Oh, I get that," I agreed. "I've always loved France, anyway. It's where my family are from originally."

"I just hopped on the first plane I could see out of there," she admitted cheerfully, and I laughed.

"You were really in that much of a rush to get out of there?"

"Wouldn't you be?" she replied, pulling a face. I supposed she had a point. We had both been in a rush, in our own ways. Ready to leave behind what we had known before. Maybe there was something to be said for that, for the freedom in just breaking out of everything you thought you had known before.

I walked her down to her place of work, and she glanced around and then darted forward to plant a quick kiss on my cheek.

"Thanks for last night," she told me, flashing me a smile. "I had a lot of fun. Maybe we could do it again sometime?"

"Maybe we could," I agreed, and her face lit up. She paused for a moment, biting her lip, as though there was something else she wanted to say to me, but she seemed to think better of it, and just hurried inside the small shop where she was going to spend the rest of her day.

I watched as she headed inside. I could smell the vanilla and baking bread from here, and it made me smile. It smelled the way that France always did in the memories I kept in my head of this place.

But now I was here, making brand new memories of my own, and I didn't want to miss out on a second to bring them to life. I was so happy, so at ease right now. I knew I would have to be careful about not letting too much slip to Oliver and Natalie, let alone Cecily, Lauren's boss, but for now, at least, I could just lose myself in the comfort of knowing I had a crush who seemed to like me just as much as I liked her.

I didn't have anything specific to do today, and I intended to spend the afternoon just wandering around the city and getting to know it a little better. I had no idea how long I was going to be here. Now that I had found Lauren, I was sure as hell in no hurry to get out of there. And if this place was going to be my home for the foreseeable future, I wanted to make the very most of it that I could.

I pondered, as I walked, on what she had told me about her life back in America. What had been so bad that she had just hopped on the first international flight out of there? What had driven her to run so far and so fast from what she had known before? Or was it just that, like me, she hadn't been able to stand the thought of being there any longer, and knew the only chance she had to keep her head on straight was to find somewhere new to start over? I had so many questions, but I knew I would have the time to find out the answers to all of them. Everything about her intrigued me, and I intended to uncover every little secret she had protected for all this time.

Maybe I could move to this place. I liked it...I liked the sound of the wind that blew down from the mountains, liked the cool air in the morning, liked the soft rain at night that seemed to pour down to take care of any sins we had been getting up to during the day. It felt different from New York in all the ways I had been hoping it would – freeing, somehow. I could exhale here everything I had been holding in when I had been back in the city, and I knew I was going to get addicted to that soon enough.

Or maybe I was just trying to come up with every excuse I could to spend more time here, because I was so far from willing to be away from Lauren. We had only just met, but there was something about her, something powerful and pulsing that, even now, wanted to pull me back in her direction. I kept my feet moving forward, salving myself with the promise it wouldn't be long until I saw her again.

And I was going to make sure of that.

10

LAUREN

"Oh, hey, Cecily," I greeted my boss, as she stepped through the front door of the small bakery shop. I didn't often see her at this end of town.

"*Bonjour,*" she replied sharply, and I felt a wash of dread run through my system. Oh, shit. Did she know? Had she figured it out somehow?

"I don't normally see you here," I replied as cheerfully as I could, shifting to close the door to the bakery behind me. I didn't want anyone else in here knowing I had a job on the side, let alone a job working for someone like her. She was a little infamous in this city, and most people who'd lived here for any length of time knew who she was, and just why she had such a reputation.

"Yes, well, I thought I would expand my palate a little," she replied, voice still icy, pointed. I kept the smile on my face. *Just don't let her see you waver.*

"And I thought, well, if this place is good enough for Victor Rousso, it's got to be good enough for me," she finished up. There it was...the killer punch. The thing that was meant to make me cringe on the spot. I tried not to react, but I was sure she spotted some of the shock on my face.

"What makes you say that?" I asked.

"I saw him here this morning," she explained, eyes piercing into mine, waiting for me to crack, waiting for me to give her something she could throw back in my face. "I remember you mentioned you worked here. I suppose you must have seen him…"

"I think I missed him," I muttered. "I work in the back most of the time."

"Well, you must have been glad to have such a wealthy client in here," she continued. My mind was racing. Had she seen him leaving me here after he had dropped me off? He had been sweet enough to offer to walk me down, and I hadn't even considered that anyone else would have seen us together. Why should I? I shouldn't have to constantly look over my shoulder and try to second-guess everything I was doing. I would have told Cecily off, warned her she was being totally invasive and she needed to back down, but I knew she would never have listened to me. Besides, I needed the job with her, and I didn't want to fuck that up so badly she would think to get rid of me. That's the last thing I needed right now.

"I guess so," I replied, trying to keep my voice bright – and failing. "Well, can I get you anything? We have other customers, and…"

She glanced around, to the empty shop, and I felt my cheeks beginning to burn. Shit. I was just making myself look like a total idiot. I tried to keep my face arranged in something that was close to normalcy. I didn't want her to guess what I had been doing with the one person she had told me to stay away from, but there was no way I was going to risk letting him slip through my fingers, either.

"I won't keep you," she replied, and with that, she turned to stalk her way out of the shop once more. I caught my breath as soon as the door shut behind her. Damn, she was on to me. And, though I knew she was being crazy, I had to be more careful.

I dived into the bakery once more, and ignored the way that Elodie was looking at me. Nobody here knew I worked at that place, too, and I wanted to keep it that way. My day-life and my nightlife were totally separate, and I intended not to let anything change that, if I could help it.

I pretended I was busy with picking up some *pain au chocolat* for the front counter and then vanished back into the shop again. Please, please, please, don't let Cecily or anyone else from my other life come in here for the rest of the day. I didn't think I could handle it. I tried to breathe in the scent of the bread baking in the next room, normally a solid salve to soothe myself. But I wasn't sure I could make it work right now.

Jesus. How quickly had she been able to catch on to what was happening in my head right now? In my life? I had to do everything I could to make sure she didn't get her hands on anything else. I had to keep away from Victor no matter what. I got the feeling Cecily was going to be stalking me from here on out to make sure I wasn't getting too closely involved with this man, and, much as I wanted nothing more than to pass a little more time with him, I knew I had to hold back.

I made it through the rest of my shift in one piece, managing to keep myself busy enough not to think too hard on everything that had happened. The last thing I needed was to allow the stress of the day to get under my skin. I had a job to do…two jobs to do, actually, since I mentioned it. And I wasn't going to let Cecily's over-involvement in what was going on outside of them get to me.

By the time I stepped out of the bakery that afternoon, I was ready to head back home and crawl into bed and get some rest before I had to turn a shift at the club that night. But instead of the peaceful quietness I had been looking forward to when I had left, I found myself confronted by the one person I knew I shouldn't have wanted to see in that moment.

"Victor!" I hissed, as soon as I saw him standing outside the bakery, leaning on the wall casually and looking for all the world as though he belonged there. "What are you doing here?"

"I checked what time the bakery closed, and I figured I would come meet you," he replied, flashing me a smile. My heart melted a little bit, even though I knew I should have known better. But there was something so impossibly sweet about the thought that he had gone out of his way to be here for me. I didn't want to let that slip through my fingers, even though I knew I should have.

"You can't be here," I told him quickly. I wanted nothing more than to invite him down to my place, to lock the door and make the most of all the time I had before I had to go back to work, but I got the feeling Cecily would be somewhere around here, and I didn't want to have to deal with what she would say to me if she saw me and this man together.

"Last I checked, the bakery isn't an invite-only club," he chuckled, pushing himself off the wall and following me as I started to make my way down the street. Should I tell him about Cecily, about what she had done to me? I doubted he would even believe me, to be honest. I didn't know what to say to him, except that he needed to stay the fuck away from me, because I didn't want to sacrifice the job I had worked so hard to get in the first place.

"I think I need to get some rest," I told him firmly, hoping he would actually listen to me. Some part of me, though, wanted him to just take control, like he had done before. I wanted him to tell me just how this was going to be, and make sure I knew I didn't have any say in it at all. But there was no way I could expect that from him. He didn't know me well enough to even think about pulling something like that, and I didn't want to put pressure on him to do something I didn't even know the depth of his experience in.

But now, I had to get rid of him. That was all that mattered. I kept walking away from him, ignoring the pulsing in my guts that told me to turn around and throw myself at him once more. And, when I looked over my shoulder once more I found that he was gone. And that was a relief, as much as it was a disappointment. I knew it was for the best. But it didn't mean I couldn't feel the keening want down inside of me, begging him to come back, begging for a release I hadn't even known I'd wanted until I had seen him again.

When I got to the club that evening, I had intended to avoid Cecily with everything that I had. I didn't want to discuss with her anything that had gone on earlier today, and even less what had happened between that man and me. I just prayed she hadn't seen us there together, but I didn't know if she would believe me if I told her that I hadn't asked him there.

I had expected her to try to stay out of my way, too, after the confrontation we'd had, but instead, she called me into the office and closed the door behind me.

"Thanks for meeting with me," she told me, and I stared at her for a moment. She was my boss. Did she really think I had any choice but to be here with her right now? If I thought that just turning around and marching out of here was an option, I would have taken it as soon as I could.

"No problem," I replied, and I glanced to the door. Suddenly, I wanted nothing more than to be out there serving drinks to perverts, as normal.

"I have something for you," she told me, and she reached into her desk. What was it, an apology? It better damn well be. I didn't want to have to tell her why her involvement in my love life was so beyond inappropriate.

But instead, she handed me a small loop of gold across the table. It had been so long since I had even thought about what they might mean that I couldn't click into what it actually was for a moment. And then, it hit me.

"Cecily, are you asking me to...?"

"I'm not asking you anything," she replied sharply. "It's tin, trust me, nothing special."

"Well, you sure do know how to make a girl feel valued," I muttered, picking up the ring and twisting it back and forth in my hand. At a glance, it could pass for a wedding ring, and I assumed that was why she had given it to me.

"I thought you might want to add something like this to your uniform," she told me, her voice ice-cold and leaving little room for debate. I eyed her for a moment.

"What do you mean?"

"I mean, just to make sure none of the men who come around here get the wrong impression of you," she pointed out. "It's an easy explanation to keep them away. And most of them won't even bother if they see you with this thing."

I stared at it for a moment. Really? She was asking me to wear a wedding ring? Was she that jealous about whatever the hell it was I had shared with Victor that she needed me to put this on? I felt like I was losing my mind. But she was my boss, and if she wanted me to wear something, then I knew there was no way I could get out of it without sounding like a total asshole.

"Sure, I'll wear it," I replied, and I slipped it on to my finger. She shook her head.

"Other hand," she told me. I winced. I hadn't even thought about putting one of these on before. I didn't even remember what I was meant to do with it. I changed the position of the ring and held out my hand in front of me. Why was it that it looked more like a shackle to me than a wedding ring? I knew people put these things on with joy in their hearts and meant every moment of it. I could never feel that way about this thing. It just felt like it was cutting off every opportunity I might have had, everything that would give me the freedom to explore and enjoy.

"That should keep the men here from getting any strange ideas about you," she remarked, and she sounded proud of the plan she had come up with. I didn't reply. Honestly, I wouldn't have minded if there was a certain man here who got the wrong idea about me. But I figured that was why she had given me this thing in the first place, because she hoped I was going to be stupid enough to drop things right then and there.

I took a deep breath before I headed out on to the floor and tried to keep my nerve, not letting the ring that was wrapped around my finger like ivy choking out a tree get under my skin. If that's what it took to keep my job, I would wear it, as simple as that. I had put up with a lot worse to keep a position, and I didn't care if this is what I had to do to hold on to this one.

Though I prayed I wasn't going to have to explain to Victor what it was doing there. And I prayed, hope against hope, that I could slip it off and into my pocket before he noticed what I was wearing.

11

VICTOR

As I closed the distance between the club and me, I found myself less excited than I had been before.

Because I couldn't stop wondering what it had been that had changed Lauren's mind about me in the time she had been at work. There was just something...when I had come to meet her again, I had been greeted by the harsh reality that she might not have wanted me as much as I wanted her, and I didn't know why the fuck that might have been.

I felt as though I was losing my mind, to be honest. Things between us had been so hot and heavy after we'd first met, and then...nothing, like I had fucked up in some irrevocable way and now I just had to figure out what I had done to make the mess that I clearly had of whatever we'd had going on.

At least I could see her again tonight. At the club. That was something, right? I had come down by myself this time, leaving behind Oliver and his wife for the time being. I just wanted some space to myself, something I could use to clear my head. And a chance to speak to Lauren on my own terms, and figure out what had happened to throw her so far from the standard we had set.

As soon as I stepped through the door, I locked eyes with her...not Lauren, but Cecily, who made her way towards me with a smile on her face like she had just been waiting for the moment I turned up once more.

"Victor, it's so good to see you," she purred, her voice low and feline. "Can I take your coat? I have a table right here that's free, perhaps you'd like to make yourself comfortable."

"Yes, thank you," I replied, and I handed her my jacket and wondered why she didn't give everyone here the same treatment.

But I already knew the answer to that question. She wasn't exactly being subtle, was she? She wanted something out of me, even if I hadn't worked out what it was yet, and I was going to have to navigate around it if I was going to get my hands on the one woman I actually wanted to see.

"Is Lauren working tonight?" I asked Cecily, figuring the best course of action was to be as blunt as possible. At least I could cut to the chase, not let her think she stood more of a chance with me than she thought she did. I knew I should have been more careful, knew perhaps I was putting Lauren's job in danger, but there was only one person I was here to see, and I wasn't going to leave until I got to lay eyes on her again.

Cecily shook her head, a brief shadow flitting over her face.

"No, she isn't," she replied, her voice taut. "She's off this evening. I suppose she needs her rest."

"I suppose so," I replied.

"And probably wants to spend time with her new husband, and all," she continued. As soon as she said those words, I felt my stomach drop to my shoes. Wait, what?

"Sorry, her new husband?" I asked her, trying to keep my voice as neutral as I possibly could and failing dismally.

"Yes, well, you know how it is with these newlyweds," she remarked, shaking her head with a chuckle. "They just want to spend all their time with one another no matter how much they have to do."

"I suppose so," I said. "When did she get married?"

"Oh, I'm not sure," she replied, waving her hand as though the thought hadn't even crossed her mind until that moment. "I didn't like to ask. But she came in wearing a wedding ring and I assumed they had finally tied the knot..."

"How long have they been together?" I asked her. She shrugged.

"I don't really know," she admitted. "Lauren likes to keep her personal life away from work. I suppose she doesn't want anyone knowing she's with someone, working at a place like this..."

My mind was racing, as I asked Cecily to get me a drink. She rushed off to do as she was told, and I thanked God she had at least given me a hot second to be all by myself. Because I had no idea what to make of the news I had just heard. Lauren was married? And they had clearly been together for a while now, if Cecily was talking about it as though their getting wed was a final situation. Shit. I didn't know how to feel about that. She had been so sweet with me, so happy to spend the night, so glad to have me walk her to work the next day.

Though, looking back, maybe that explained her snap-change in attitude when I had come to see her the afternoon post-work. Perhaps she had been able to write it off as some sort of fling, a one-time thing she would never have to follow up on again. And seeing me there had been a reminder that she had done wrong and there was no hiding from that fact.

Shit. Had I just rolled into bed with a married woman? How recently had she gotten married? Because I was pretty sure I hadn't seen a ring on her finger when we had been fucking. I would have noticed something like that. Of course she didn't have it on...no doubt she would have cast that off as soon as she saw me and decided she wanted to get me into bed. No way she would let her real life get in the way of something exciting like that, would she?

Fucking hell. I took a long sip of the drink Cecily had one of her waitresses deliver, and stared at the polished wood table in front of me. I felt...Jesus, I didn't even know. Angry? Yeah, sure. But hurt, too. I had really thought we had some sort of connection going on, but clearly, she only had that with her husband. I was just some guy for her to use in the meantime, to take up the space when she wanted something a little more fun, a little more exciting. I hated her in that moment, I really did.

And yet I knew if she had walked through that door right here and now, I would have been utterly hopeless to resist her. I wanted to get my hands on her again. Maybe even teach her a lesson about lying to me. Yeah, I could see her now, eyes shining with playfulness, as she stared up at me, telling me she was willing to do anything to make it up to me.

No. No. I couldn't let thoughts like that get into my head. I needed to keep pushing forward, keeping pushing on without her. As much as I was tempted to just let myself slip backwards into the desire I had for her, the last thing I needed on earth right now was someone getting under my skin, inside my head, making me overthink in a way that I couldn't undo. I was here for business, not pleasure, and that had been the case since this had all started. I wasn't going to let anything change that.

But I didn't see much point in sticking around here if the one woman I had been hoping to run into was nowhere to be seen. I might as well head home and get a good night's rest and be done with all of this, once and for all. I wasn't going to do myself any good sitting around and drinking hard and waking up with a hangover tomorrow.

Not when I knew that her presence wouldn't be there to take the edge off of it. Not yet. Not so soon.

12

LAUREN

As I slipped out of the back of the club to catch my breath, I pulled the ring off my finger and stuffed it in my pocket for a moment. I didn't want to have to look at it for another moment. I hated this fucking thing. I hated what it had come to represent, and I hated, most of all, how stupid I felt when I was wearing it.

I was never going to get married. Never. Not if it brought me everything this fucking ring had told me it would. Everyone was suddenly only interesting in asking about my husband, and I didn't see how I was meant to play off the questions without giving away the fact I was faking it. Even to the other members of staff, I had to play along, and I didn't know how long Cecily was going to make me do this. Plenty of other women worked here, women who she hadn't landed with the shackle of this ring...so why me?

I knew the answer to that question. She wanted to make sure I didn't get a chance to go near the man she clearly had her eye on. I hadn't seen him at the club in the last few days, and I wondered if perhaps Victor Rousso had already decided to head home again. Was I a part of that choice? I had no idea if he had heard about my so-called wedding, and frankly, I wasn't that much interested in finding out, either. The humiliation of having him thinking I had been cheating on my husband with him...no. There was no way I could handle that. Not a chance in hell.

I inhaled deeply, the vague smell of dish soap and wine from the kitchen flooding out into the small alleyway behind the club. I knew I would need to go back to work soon, but I didn't want to. There was something about watching the performers playing this evening that made it hard for me to focus. I couldn't stop thinking about what it might have been like if Victor had been the one playing with me, how good it might have felt to have his hands around me, to feel him inside of me.

And instead, I just had to go about my job as though nothing was different. Even though I knew everything was. How the hell was I supposed to keep my head on straight when all I could think about was how much I wanted him, and how difficult Cecily was going to make it for me to have him once more?

Shit. There was no point standing around here feeling sorry for myself. I had to get back to business. Where was a cigarette when you needed one? I had quit years ago, but I felt like I could have used a quick draw right now...

"Lauren."

But before I could vanish back to work once more, a voice caught my attention. A voice that made everything around me slow down for a moment, a voice that made my heart start to beat double-time inside my chest. I turned, and saw him standing there...the man I hadn't been able to get out of my head, the man who probably thought I had been using him to cheat on my so-called husband.

"Victor," I breathed, and I glanced around to make sure nobody was watching us. If I was out here for more than a few minutes, I knew someone would notice and come out to check on me, and if they found me with this man, then there was going to be hell to pay.

He didn't wait for me to say another word. He just moved towards me, kissed me hard, pushed me back against the rain-slicked wall behind us. I didn't wait for him to explain himself. I didn't need him to. When his mouth was on mine like that, when his body was pressed up against mine, everything else seemed to slip out of my head. Including the fact that my very boss had told me I should keep my hands off of him at any cost. That she didn't want me anywhere near him.

"You're mine," he breathed into my ear, and I nodded.

"Yes," I murmured back to him, and he pulled back, looked me dead in the eye, and grasped my chin in his hand so he could turn my head to look at him.

"You belong to me," he told me, his voice edged with a sureness that made something stir in the base of my spine. I nodded again.

"Say it," he ordered me, and this time, I knew he wasn't going to give me what I needed until I spoke the words out loud.

"I belong to you," I breathed, and he kissed me again – this time, with the kind of passion that knocked the breath right out of my lungs. How could I think about anything else? How could I even pretend there was any other want inside of me? I needed him. I had needed him since the moment I had last seen him outside the bakery, when he had come all the way down there to see me. I had needed him then and I needed him now and I didn't care what anyone else thought of it. I just wanted to be with him, and, for now, it seemed, he just wanted to be with me.

He scooped me off the ground so I could wrap my legs around him, and pinned my arms to the wall behind me. Not that I had any intention of fighting with him. All I could focus on was the pressure of his cock against me down below, how much I wanted him inside of me. And how amazed I was that he could just treat me like this and make me believe every single moment of it, even though we were far from the toys and whips and chains that lived back inside the club.

He pulled my panties down, ripped them off in one swift motion, and stuffed them deep into my mouth to keep me quiet. I could hardly control myself. I didn't know what he was going to do next, but I was sure I was going to love every moment of it. How could I not? The lust he sent through me was crazy, that passion more than I could take. If there was ever anything that measured up to this...

"Keep quiet," he ordered me, as he unzipped his pants and pulled a condom from his pocket. His strength kept me pinned in place, his power making it impossible for me to even wriggle playfully. And that was just how I wanted it. It was as though all the breath had been knocked out of my lungs; all I could think about was the way he was holding me in place, how badly I wanted him inside of me in that moment. I needed to feel his fullness the way I had before, or else nothing was going to count.

He lowered his voice, pressed his mouth against my ear, and planted his cock at the entrance to my pussy.

"Tell me you want this," he ordered me. I opened my mouth, trying to find the words, but I didn't even know where to start.

"Tell me," he ordered me, and he pushed himself just an inch inside of me, making me groan.

"I need this," I begged with him, through the fabric of the panties. "Please, Victor, please..."

"Good girl," he murmured back, and, with that, he pushed up and inside of me in one swift motion. And I felt my body go limp as the pleasure took control of me.

There was nothing like the sensation of being penetrated for the first time. My pussy stretching to accommodate his cock, to take his full length, that deep fullness that came with being taken in this way. I buried my head into his shoulder, worried the panties might not be enough to keep me quiet.

He moved into me in long, hard strokes, probably knowing as well as I did that there was no way we could hold back or wait around right now. We had to just give in to this sensation, to the want of it, to the way that it felt. We could have been caught at any moment, but I still knew there was no way I was going to be able to hold off on the way this made me feel. Even if the entire staff of the club had walked out of there at once to watch me do this, I couldn't have stopped. I was in it now, or he was in me, and that was all I could focus on. All that mattered to me, deep down.

"Fuck," he groaned into my ear, and that brief moment of his loss of control was enough to make my entire body quake for a second. I wrapped one arm around his back and sank my nails against his skin. I needed to feel him, I needed feel everything I possibly could from him, and then it might be enough for me to let him go. I wanted to indulge myself in every way I could and tell him everything I wanted to, tell him everything that had been on my mind, but I didn't even know where to begin.

Especially not when I could already feel the orgasm that was rising up inside of me begin to dull my senses and my ability to think. My body was beginning to tense, find its structure again, and he planted a kiss against my neck, his mouth warm on my skin. I arched my back to push myself back against him, tipping my head back and letting the first few drops of the evening rain brush over my skin. Yes. This moment, right here. This was what I had been waiting for. This was what I had needed, with everything inside of me. Not some fake husband, but this real man, this real man who took control like he knew he was owed it.

Was this really happening? I would have thought I had conjured him from a dream or something like that, but I knew a dream could never have felt as real as this. I pressed my head against him and breathed in his scent, promised myself this was real...this was really happening...and I closed my eyes and let everything else go.

And that's when it hit me.

The orgasm burst through me like someone had pulled the pin on a grenade, my body tensing around his like it was trying to catch him in a vise-grip. I didn't care. I groaned, tipped my head back, let the pressure finally flow out of me. I knew there was nothing more than this moment right now. I couldn't control the way it felt, but I knew I would come back to it a million times over, trying to make sense of it, trying to make sense of the way it made me feel and knowing it would be impossible to wrap my head around it anytime soon.

The panties muffled my cries, but if they hadn't been there, I was pretty sure everyone in the club would have come running. I didn't care. My pussy pulsed with the relief of the release he had given me, and he held himself inside of me, allowing me to milk him dry of everything he had for a few more moments. It didn't take long until I felt his cock twitch inside of me, fill me, his body shaking for a split-second as he held on to me for dear life.

That was the most addictive part of all of this. Knowing that, for all his strength, for all his sureness, I could be enough to strip him back to his bare essentials for a moment. It might not have been much, but it was something, that inch of power I could pry back from him, and I would take it. I would take it every way I could get it. I didn't care how long it took me to find this moment again, all I cared about was the helpless, hopeless thrill of being his, and knowing that our bodies matched each other as well as they did. I was falling for him, hopelessly, I couldn't stop it, and I barely knew him. It was just that I had never met anyone who made me feel the way he did, and the addiction was already too much for me to hide from.

He planted me back down on my feet, my legs shaking so

much it was a miracle I managed to stay upright. He hooked my panties out of my mouth and stuffed them into his pocket.

"Back to work," he told me, and I nodded. I didn't have it in me to argue with him. How could I? All I wanted right now was to please him, and I was pretty sure I had done just that. For now, for the time being, all I was focused on was making sure I did just what I was told when the orders came out of his mouth. Because if this was my reward, then it was worth it every step of the way.

I pulled my skirt down, trying to ignore the wetness on the inside of my thighs that I knew was going to be a delicious discomfort all night long. As soon as I closed the door behind me, Annie, one of the other waitresses, looked over at me with a frown on her face.

"Are you alright?" she asked me. "You were out there for a while."

"Yeah, I'm fine," I promised her, and I smoothed my hair back from my head and tried to keep the big-ass grin off my face. "Anyway. We should be getting back to work, right?"

"Yeah, we should," she agreed, and her words were pointed. I didn't care. I couldn't have cared less if she had dropped a whole tray of drinks on the floor in front of me and told me to clean the whole thing up. Right now, the only thing I was thinking about was the man who had just manifested from the dark to be with me...and how long I was going to have to wait to have him like that again.

13

VICTOR

"So, I think we have a deal," Oliver remarked brightly, a smile spreading over his face from the other side of his office table. I nodded.

"I think we do," I agreed. I knew I should have been happier about all of this, but there was something nagging at the back of my mind, something I couldn't shake, and it was making it hard to focus on anything else.

"I'm so glad you're going to be investing with us," Oliver continued, rising to his feet and tucking the papers we had just agreed on back into his bag so he could take them down to his lawyer to look over.

"Me too," I agreed. "This place is great, really."

"Oh, you don't have to convince me of that," he chuckled, and, for a moment, he eyed me, as though there was something he wanted to say. I looked back at him expectantly.

"Something on your mind?"

"Something on yours?" he shot back. I sighed and pulled on my jacket once more. So, I hadn't been able to hide the fact there was a woman in my head that I couldn't get rid of.

"I guess there is," I admitted. "Can I ask you something?"

"With the money you just invested in our business, you can ask me anything," he replied, slapping me on the shoulder as we headed out of his office. "What's on your mind?"

"What's the deal with marriage here?" I asked him. He cocked his head to the side and gave me a funny look.

"What do you mean?"

"Is it common for people to have open marriages?" I wondered aloud. He furrowed his brow for a moment, as though scanning the depths of his experience, and then he shook his head.

"Not that I know of," he replied. "Even people in the scene, they tend to be pretty possessive of what's theirs, even if they're willing to show it off. Why do you ask?"

"I think I might have accidentally gotten involved with a married woman," I admitted, and his eyebrows shot up so high they nearly vanished into his hairline.

"I think you need to tell me everything," he remarked, and he guided me through to the tasting room, where he poured me a generous glass of wine from the decanter. I took it, looked down into the silky red depths, and wondered what the hell to do next.

"There's a woman," I confessed. "We've only hooked up a few times."

"Did you know she was married when all of this started?" he asked, and I shook my head at once.

"No, and if I had known, I wouldn't have gone near her," I replied. "I've never been with a married woman before, and it's not something I ever really wanted for myself. I thought it was too much complication, you know, too much for me to handle, and I always just thought that it seemed...cruel. To the man in question..."

"Yeah, I can see that," he agreed, taking a long sip of the wine that he had poured for himself. "But the question is, does she want to be married still?"

"I guess if she's sleeping with me, then she must want out of it," I replied. "At least, that's what I assume. But I don't know why she would try to hide it from me if that was the case. Just seems needlessly stressful for everyone involved."

"Including you," he pointed out. "Has she come to you, or do you go to her?"

I thought back to the night before, turning up at the club, slipping around the back in the hopes of finding a staff entrance so I could find Lauren. And, sure enough, there she had been, no wedding ring, dressed in a short skirt with her hair pulled back and looking like a slice of pure heaven. And yeah, it was fair to say that I had gone seeking that out for myself, because I couldn't resist the thought of getting my hands on her again.

And she had told me she belonged to me. I could still hear her words in my ear, though muffled by the panties I had stuffed into her mouth. She had told me she belonged to me without a second thought, and that she was mine, and she had let me fuck her right there and then as though I was the only one she wanted to be with.

But Cecily had told me that she was married, and I didn't know what to make of it. There was no reason for her boss to lie about something as big as that. I might have had issues with the way that Cecily seemed to attach herself to me, but the thought of someone making up something as huge as that was just ridiculous even in theory. Nobody would have gone that far just to stake a claim.

Would they?

"So what are you going to do about it?" he asked me. I shook my head.

"I have no idea," I admitted. "I don't know what I can do."

"Let her come to you," he suggested. "If she's really not interested in carrying on that marriage anymore, then she'll make that clear somehow."

"But what am I meant to do in the meantime?" I asked him. "Just wait?"

"There's plenty you can do to fill the time," he replied. "Why don't we go to the club tonight? That will get your mind off it."

"I guess," I muttered. He had no idea, of course, that the very woman who was the cause of all of my problems happened to work there, but I had no intention of telling him, either. I wanted to keep this all wrapped up and close to my chest for now. It just seemed to make more sense that way. I didn't want to complicate their lives by getting them involved in the mess I had managed to make with the woman I couldn't stop thinking about.

And besides...right now, I would take any excuse I could, to get inside the club again.

I went home and showered, then changed, and then met Oliver again to head down to the Petit Mort. He claimed we were celebrating our newly made deal, and I wondered if I should tell him the truth, that there was another reason I had decided to come down here today.

But for now, it was better to let him think he understood what I was doing here. I scanned the room as soon as I stepped through the door, and sure enough, there she was...Lauren. Looking like a gift wrapped up in a tight pencil skirt and a button-down blouse that were just waiting to be ripped right off her body.

And then, I saw it...for the first time, I actually saw it. Glinting in the light, as though the universe was trying to guide my attention in its direction. The ring on her finger. Shining. A circle that looped around her hand, a promise that she had made to someone who wasn't me.

A promise I had helped her break. Over and over again.

I tore my gaze away from her before she had a chance to look around and see me standing there. I didn't want her serving me tonight. The temptation to lay my hands on her would have been far too strong, and I couldn't resist it right now.

Cecily headed over to the table as soon as she saw us arrive, and my heart sank. I didn't want to have to deal with her right now, but I got the feeling she would do anything to get her hands on my attention for the time being. I managed to mark out a smile on my face, and Oliver rose to his feet to greet her, as though he could sense how little I wanted to talk to her and was deflecting for me before she had a chance to get close.

"It's wonderful to see you here again so soon," she told me, sliding into the seat beside me.

"Well, we're celebrating tonight," Oliver explained to her. "We just signed a deal for Victor to invest in our vineyard."

"Oh, that's wonderful news!" Cecily exclaimed, a smile spreading over her face. "We must get a bottle of champagne for you."

Before I could stop her, she had raised a hand to draw the attention of the nearest server who, of course, just so happened to be Lauren. I winced as she came over to the table, doing her best to avoid my gaze.

"Bring us a bottle of champagne," Cecily ordered her, not taking her eyes off me. "We're celebrating tonight."

"Of course," Lauren replied, and for the briefest moment, our eyes locked. And I was sure, in that instant, I could see something she was trying to keep under wraps...the desire that we had shared the night before last, when I had come down here to take her all over again. I knew it wouldn't slip from her memory so easily, nor did I want it to. I knew it was greedy, but I wanted to be on her mind. I wanted to be the only thing in her head, even when she went home to that husband of hers.

She returned with the champagne and the glasses, and her hand skimmed over my arm for the briefest instant as she planted my glass down in front of me. That act of service was enough to stir something inside of me, a passion I had been trying to ignore. I couldn't act on it. Not here. Not now. Even though I wanted nothing more than to pull her into my lap and show her just how hard a time I'd been having getting her out of my head.

"Well, congratulations on your new deal," Cecily remarked, as she poured us all a glass and then lifted hers.

"Yes, I think we have good reason to celebrate," Oliver agreed. He sounded a little clunky, clearly not sure what to say to Cecily now that she seemed to have impinged on our night. Maybe he thought she was the married woman I was doing my very best to get into bed with again. Jesus, I couldn't think of much worse than that. Cecily wasn't an unattractive woman, but she did nothing for me. Maybe it was her constant forwardness, the way she had pushed herself into my line of sight from the very first second she had laid eyes on me with one thing in mind the whole time.

We sipped on the champagne and made polite conversation, and Cecily pressed herself against me enthusiastically as though she was trying to tell me something I had never wanted to hear from her. My eyes were drawn to Lauren, again and again, though she was clearly going out of her way to avoid even looking at me. Could she feel it, too? She must have been able to feel it. Even here, even now, even when we knew we should have been hiding what we felt for one another, it was impossible to deny it.

"I think I'd like to give you a tour of our playrooms," Cecily announced to me, once she had sipped down a couple of glasses of champagne and seemed to have opened up her confidence a little.

"I think I've seen plenty of them," I tried to protest, but Oliver kicked me under the table and raised his eyebrows at me. I glanced over at him, not sure, for a moment, what he was getting at. And then it hit me. He thought he was helping. He thought I needed to get my mind off whatever woman I had stuck in there right now, and Cecily was giving me that chance.

"Just a tour," she replied, and she rose to her feet. "The second one from the left has some fascinating pieces in it; I'd love to show you around."

And before I could tell her no again, she was gone, and I knew there would be no way for me to get out of this. Oliver grinned at me.

"You know what they say, don't you?" he remarked. "Best way to get over someone."

"I'm not looking to get over anyone," I replied, a little more sharply than I had intended, and I found my gaze drawn in Lauren's direction once more. She wasn't even looking at me. She was busy, catching up with all the work she had to take care of. And I was going to have to deal with her boss, one way or the other, whether I wanted to or not. And I sincerely wished that the answer was not.

After a few minutes, I tossed back the last of my champagne and rose to my feet. I needed to make it clear to Cecily I had no interest in her like that. She was an attractive woman, sure, and I admired what she had built here, but I didn't want anything else from her. I was already running through everything I planned to say in my head.

And that's when I opened the door, and saw the very last thing on the other side that I had wanted to.

"Shit!" I exclaimed, averting my eyes at once. It was Cecily. She had, somehow, managed to bind herself to the bed, wrapping restraints around her wrists so she was all laid out and on display for me. And yeah, every inch of her was on display, too.

She was naked, totally bare-ass naked, and had arched her back theatrically from the bed, her lips parted as though there was so much she wanted to say to me that she didn't know where to start.

"Is this how you want me?" she breathed to me, and her voice was such a vague stab at seductive I almost laughed. I didn't know what to say or do. I needed her to get some fucking clothes on, and then we could take it from there.

"Cecily, no," I replied, and I averted my eyes from her as I reached down to toss the covers on the bed over her body. I didn't want to have to look at her. I didn't want to have to see her like this. I could already feel that awful second-hand humiliation, and I knew this was going to be a serious kick to her ego, but she shouldn't have gone out on such a limb when I had been giving her signs from the moment I had met her that I wanted nothing to do with her like this.

"Are you really telling me that you don't want me?" she purred, trying awkwardly to kick the covers away from her body. I nodded at once.

"Cecily, I'm not interested in you like this."

"That's fine," she replied at once, and she clicked something that released the bonds she had wrapped herself up in. Propping herself up on the bed, she grabbed my arm and pushed me down.

"I'm a switch," she explained. "I can top for you, if you prefer that."

"No, you're not listening to me," I told her, shaking my head. "I don't want any of this with you."

"What are you talking about?" she asked, and, for the first time since this whole mess had started, I began to see the sureness in her face begin to falter. I didn't want to have to do this to her, but if she wasn't going to listen to me, I didn't see how else I could do it.

"I'm not looking for anything sexual with you," I told her, and I sat up on the bed and handed her the covers. She wrapped them around her shoulders at once, looking as though she was going to cry. I hated to see such a strong woman so broken.

"I'm...it's not the right time for me," I told her. It was basically a white lie, something that was meant to make her feel better about the fool she had just made of herself, but it was the best I could offer her right now. It might not be much, but it was something. Honestly, I was still getting over the shock of seeing her bare-ass naked in front of me, clearly so sure she was going to get everything she wanted from me any way she would have liked it.

"I think I should go," I said, and I rose to my feet once more. She grabbed on to my hand again.

"No, please stay," she replied, her voice edged with desperation. "We can talk. It's fine. I can figure this out."

"There's nothing to figure out," I reminded her, and, with that, I stepped out of the door and closed it behind me.

I leaned up against it for a moment and tried to catch my breath. I didn't know what the hell that woman had been thinking, but I felt seriously bad for her that I had given her the vibes for a moment that would have led her to believe all of this was what I wanted.

Because there was only one woman I wanted to be locked inside one of those rooms with. And she was here tonight, but she wouldn't even look at me if she could avoid it. And I knew there was more of a mess there than there was in the room I had just walked out of.

I made my way back to the table where Oliver was, and prayed he wasn't going to ask what had happened there. I didn't have the heart to tell him the truth. I didn't want to humiliate Cecily further than I already had. I knew she would be licking her wounds over this for a long time, and frankly, that was the last thing I needed to concern myself with now.

I just picked up the bottle of champagne and poured myself another generous glass. I took a long sip and slumped into the booth once more. And I prayed that Cecily would have gotten the message I didn't want anything to do with her.

14

LAUREN

"No way," I giggled, as Annie and I shared a smoke outside the back of the kitchen. It had been a long time since I'd smoked, but something about the stress of the situation that had arisen with the man I just couldn't get out of my head seemed to call for it.

"I mean, I don't know for sure, you can't trust everything that Franc says," she replied, as she let out a plume of smoke into the street around us. It was strange to think I had snuck out here just a few days ago, been pinned against that wall, and let a man take me as though he owned every inch of me and always had. Even now, I couldn't help but shiver at the thought of it, and wished he would emerge from the dark once more.

"No, but she was really naked?" I asked. A little gossip had been passed around the kitchen from the night before. Apparently, Cecily had been seen making a run for it from one of the playrooms with nothing but a sheet draped around her shoulders, towards her office. Nobody seemed to know who she had been in there with, but they had clearly left her in the lurch, and everyone was trying to work out just what might have happened to cause her to get caught out in such a way.

But I had a feeling I already knew the answer to that question. Because there was only one man in this town who I could think of who could have caused a woman like that to make such a fool of herself.

And he was the very same man who had fucked me against the wall just a few nights before.

"I didn't even know she was into that stuff," Annie said, as she stubbed out her cigarette on the wall and dropped it into the trashcan beside us.

"I guess you'd have to be, to run a place like this," I remarked.

"I've never really thought about it," Annie admitted. Annie was a little older than me, and had worked here longer than I had, but nothing seemed to catch her off-guard these days. She had been at this place for long enough, I supposed, that she had seen most everything they could throw at us.

"Well, I better get back to work," she remarked cheerfully. "You want to come in?"

"No, I'm going to finish this, and then I'll be right there," I replied, holding up the last inch or so of the cigarette I had before I was done. It had been such a long time since I'd had one of these, I had almost forgotten just how rough they could be on you.

Speaking of rough. As I stood there, in the cool, clear evening, trying to avoid going back inside to work once more, I wondered if he was thinking of me, too. I had no idea where Victor was or what he might have been doing, but I'd guess he planned to avoid the club as best he could for the foreseeable future, given that my boss had thrown herself full force in his direction the night before.

If that was what had really happened. I had no proof of it, of course, but I was getting surer and surer this was the only explanation for Cecily's being caught out like that. The question was, of course, why the hell she had decided this was the way it was going to go. Why she had locked her sights on him to the exclusion of nearly every other man in the city. I knew there were plenty of men who would have done anything to get their hands on her any way she wanted them, and yet...

And yet, Victor was the man she wanted. Was it about money? It had to be, right? There was no other explanation for how certain she seemed to be about what she wanted from him. But she was a wealthy woman, thanks to running this club for as long as she had, and I couldn't imagine she needed to attach herself to a man like him just to make sure she got everything she wanted from her life.

But she had made sure to get in the way of whatever we had going on, put that ring on my finger and no doubt lit it with a big, flashing light every time he was around. I hadn't had time to ask him, the last time we had been together, if he knew about the husband I allegedly had, but he must have. He had talked to me like he wanted me to know that he owned me, through and through, and I didn't know what else that could have been alluding to than the man I certainly had never married in the first place.

I stubbed out the cigarette and tossed the rest of it away. I knew if I finished it, I was only going to wake up in pain tomorrow, and I could do without that right now.

It was strange, really, because I had been craving pain ever since the last time Victor and I had fucked. It was something I had never ached for like this before, something I had never needed in this deep, profound way...something that seemed to make my skin ache and my body cry out for more, more than I had ever had before in my life.

Watching the performers that night, a femdom scene, a woman with a paddle making a man count the blows out one by one as she landed them on his ass, I found myself wondering just how much I could have taken. How much I would be willing to take, if the time came. I didn't know how far I could go, and I didn't know if I could ever even want that from someone who wasn't Victor.

I went through the rest of my shift keeping an eye pinned to the door to see if he was going to turn up, but there was nothing. Nobody. He wasn't here, and I would have been surprised if he was coming back at all. I had heard he was celebrating something last night, maybe celebrating the fact he could finally go back home once more. I was curious, but it wasn't like I could ask without attracting some of the wrong kind of attention.

But, before I was due to head home, Annie waved me down from her spot at the hostess counter, and I headed over to see what she wanted. I assumed, honestly, that she was just wondering when we could slip out for another cigarette, but instead, she pushed a card into my hand.

"Someone dropped this off for you," she told me, clearly already distracted by the new group who was arriving even as we spoke.

"Who?" I asked curiously, looking down at the paper she had given me. She shrugged.

"I didn't recognize him," she replied, but then, Annie had always had a dreadful eye for faces. I looked down at the card, trying to keep it concealed, trying to hide the excitement that was written all over my face as I prayed, prayed, prayed...

And then I saw his name, written in ink, smudged slightly from where I was sure it had been in his pocket, and I smiled. It was an address. His address. He must have known we couldn't keep doing what we were doing here. We had to find quieter ways to sneak around.

My heart was pounding as I tucked it into my pocket, and I struggled to keep the smile of my face as I returned to work. I knew this was going to get me in one whole hell of a lot of trouble. But it was hard to care when all I could think about were his hands on my body once more. I wanted to find out how much I could take? Well, I was going to know by the time the night was done. And I could hardly wait to discover just what he had in store for me.

15

VICTOR

I STOOD THERE, OUTSIDE THE BAKERY, AND I KNEW THAT WHAT I was about to do could land me in one whole hell of a lot of trouble if I wasn't careful right now.

But I was tired of being careful. After what we had been through last night, I didn't want another inch of careful in my life. I just wanted her. And I wasn't going to be able to stop until I knew I had her.

When she had turned up at my hotel room, I had opened the door before she could knock on it. She stood there before me, her eyes wide, as though she couldn't quite believe this was actually happening.

"Victor," she murmured, but I covered her mouth with my hand and pulled her inside. If someone worked out she was here, then I was going to be in some serious trouble. I knew that the two of us being together like this was probably dangerous, but that just made it all the more exciting.

I knew she was always going to take me up on my invitation. How could she not? After everything we had been through, the tension between us had just grown beyond the point where I could take it anymore. Her boss might have been throwing herself at me, but there was only one woman I truly wanted and, as I pushed her down on to the bed, I knew I couldn't deny my feelings for her any longer.

"Victor, we need to talk," she said, but I just kissed her. Talking wasn't at the top of my plans right now. She wrapped her arms around me and moaned against my mouth, and I knew she felt just the same way. There was plenty for us to say to one another when this was all over, once we had put it all behind us, once we had managed to push away the desire that consumed us both when we were together.

When she spoke again, she had different plans in mind.

"I want you to tie me up," she whispered. "Please. I can't stop. I feel like I've been so out-of-control. I just need to be controlled for a while."

"Anything the lady wants," I promised her at once, my cock already stirring at the thought of having her bound in front of me. She was right. We had both been out of control for a while now. The best way to fix that was to pull ourselves back into each other, to feel that orbit connect and for our paths to match again.

I managed to dig out some silk ties from the drawers filled with my clothes...not much, but it was something to work with, at least. I wrapped one around her wrists, tying them together and then binding them to the headboard above her, and then I looped another around her head, letting it come to rest in her mouth so she was biting down on it, starving for it.

I leaned back for a moment to admire my handiwork, and God did she look hot like that. I leaned down over her, knowing I was in complete and utter control of her right now.

"You look perfect," I said, and she groaned against the binding. I began to strip her down, peeling off the clothes she had worn to her shift at work that day, stripping her almost naked so I could take in every single inch of her. God, was there anything better than this? I brushed my lips over her neck, pushing my hand into her panties as I went. She was already wet. Soaked. She moaned and pushed her hips back up to meet me, and I looked down on her with a smile on my face. I could have done anything I wanted to her in that moment, and it was tempting to just get up and walk away right now, to leave her writhing and pleading for me to give her something more. But my cock was already hard, and I needed to be inside her right now before I lost control entirely.

I unzipped my pants and pulled my cock into my hand, and leaned back to look at her, pumping my erection a few times to bring it to full hardness. Her nipples were swollen, her chest rising and falling rapidly, her legs shaking with need. She was gazing at me with a pleading expression on her face, begging me every way she knew how to give her what she wanted.

"You want me to fuck you?" I asked her. I knew what her answer was going to be, but it was still gratifying to hear her plead for it through the gag in her mouth.

"I don't think I can hear you," I teased her, moving up on top of her, pulling her panties aside so my fingers were hovering just an inch above her pussy. "Do you want me to fuck you, or not?"

She nodded again, her eyes written with a keen desperation that I just loved to see on her. That was all I needed to see. I planted my cock at the entrance to her pussy, and watched as her whole body convulsed as I pushed myself inside of her.

She cried out, and I leaned down to wrap my arms around her, letting my hands roam across her body unhindered. There was something so incredibly hot to me about having her like this, about knowing she belonged to me. That she would do anything to be with me. I knew she could have gotten fired for this, but she didn't care. When I made her feel this good, why should she?

I slammed myself into her in long, hard strokes, the same

ones I'd wanted to give her all day long. If there was a time when I would get tired of having her in my head, in my bed, I hoped that we would never get there. I just wanted to keep losing myself to her. I wanted to feel like there was nothing else in this world but the two of us. The fire I felt when I was inside of her, the burning want that consumed my body, it made everything else vanish and fall away. This woman did more for me than anyone else I had ever been with. And I was never going to let her go.

Her pussy was tight and slick around my cock and I didn't hold back as I filled her, over and over again. She drew her legs back so I could slide deeper inside of her, and hooked her ankles around my back, a small piece of control that she could wrestle back from me. I let her have it. Teasing her with these moments that she thought she owned me, this was the best part, and I sure as hell wasn't going to miss out on it.

It didn't take long until I could feel my balls tingling, my seed boiling inside of me as it ached to fill her. I looked into her eyes again, pushing her hair back from her face so that I meet her gaze properly, and I could tell that she was close, too. Just the way I wanted her. I slowed a little, teasing this moment out a little longer, but I couldn't hold myself back. I kissed her again, and as soon as I felt her warm mouth against mine, it happened.

I couldn't help but cry out when I came. The feeling of filling her like this was just so fucking good. I needed it. Needed every moment of it I could get. How the hell was I supposed to let her just stroll off back to work, know I could barely look at her without reliving this moment inside my head? Husband or not, I didn't care. She was mine. She would always been mine. And she knew that, just as well as I did.

I held myself deep inside of her, and, a few moments later, I felt her pussy start to contract around my cock as the orgasm rushed through her once more. I pulled back to stare into her eyes, and I swear, the look she was giving me right now was everything I needed from her. It was helpless, hopeless, impossible to contain, as though everything was building to this moment...as though she had set foot outside of the club and known this was where the rest of the night was going to take her.

And, as I kissed her again, not caring about the binding in her mouth, I held her close. Because I was only just getting started.

And, just as I thought we would, we spent the entire night together. Getting to know one another inside and out. I didn't mention her husband, and she didn't bring him up, and I assumed that she had long since forgotten about him. *Good.* That was how I wanted it. I wanted him out of her head, as long as she was with me.

But when I woke the next morning, she was gone, and I couldn't for the life of me figure out where the hell she had gotten to. And then I remembered. I remembered where she had told me she worked other than the club. She was at the bakery. That place had pulled her away from me.

And it was then it clicked. I had to do something about it. I had no idea what that something might look like, but I needed to find a way to make sure she would never have to worry about the job slipping through her fingers, no matter how long she spent curled up in bed with me after we had finished fucking.

Which meant I needed to take control of that place. For good. I needed to buy it.

I couldn't believe a thought as crazy as that had actually crossed my mind, but there it was. The shock of it was almost more than I could take, but I knew I was right. I was looking for business deals here, and I didn't know what else I was supposed to do to make this happen...to make sure I could get as much of her as I could while I was here. Aside from buying Petit Mort, which I knew Cecily was never going to part with, anyway...this was the next best thing.

Which was how I found myself standing outside the bakery where she worked, wondering just what in the hell I was doing... and just how mad she was going to be when she figured out what I had done. I took my time before I entered the shop, not even sure if she would be working there this late into the afternoon. I had spent a while calling my lawyers back in the US and I knew I had to get everything in place before I could even think about pitching an idea as huge as this one.

Maybe Lauren would think I was crazy. Shit, maybe I was a little crazy for thinking this was the way to go about things. She had asked me to take some control from her, but was this over the line...?

There was only one way for me to find out, and that was if I took a step through the door and figured out, one way or another, what the owners of this place were going to say.

But, as soon as I stepped inside, I saw her standing there and she was talking to a man. A man who, it seemed, she was pretty damn happy to see.

I felt something inside me curl up in anger, something I shouldn't have been paying any attention to. And with that, I strode towards the counter so I could talk to her. Because I had a whole fucking lot on my mind right now.

16

LAUREN

As soon as I saw him storming into the bakery, my heart sank. Because I knew this was going to be some serious trouble.

"What are you doing here?" I demanded, glancing around to make sure nobody else on shift with me had seen him come in. The guy who I had been serving looked around to see what had drawn my attention, and when he saw the look on Victor's face, he backed off quickly.

"Is that him?" he asked, jabbing his finger in the direction of the man I had just been talking to.

"Is that who?" I asked, shaking my head at him. "Victor, you know you can't be in here. If..."

"If, what, your husband finds out about us?" he demanded. I could hear the hurt in his voice, but I couldn't reply for a moment. Shit. What was he talking about?

"What do you mean?" I hissed, lowering my voice and hoping he would follow suit. He didn't.

"Is that your husband?" he demanded. I shook my head.

"I have no idea what you're talking about, but no, that isn't my husband," I snapped back at him. Thank God he was speaking in English and most of the people in this store wouldn't have been able to translate. The last thing I needed was for news of this to spread around and for people to start asking questions about just what I might have been hiding.

"So, where is he?" he asked, tossing his hands in the air. "And how long 'til you actually broached the subject of him with me?"

"For one, it's not like you gave me much of a chance to talk last night," I reminded him. "And for another, I don't have a husband! I have nothing to tell you about!"

He fell silent, thank goodness. But he looked even more confused than he had before.

"What are you talking about?"

"I could ask you the same thing," I fired back. "Where did you get the idea I had a husband?"

"I saw you with the ring on when you were at the club," he pointed out. "And Cecily told me..."

As soon as I heard that name come out of his mouth, it all started to click into place for me. That was why Cecily had given me the wedding ring. She had wanted to make sure I didn't get any closer to the man she so clearly had her eye on. My jaw dropped as it all started to fall into place, my mind piecing everything together so fast that it became a blur inside my head.

"Cecily told you that I was married?" I asked, and he nodded.

"Yeah, she did," he replied, and he crossed his arms over his chest. "And you're telling me that's not true?"

"Look, do you see a ring on this finger?" I asked him, flashing him the hand that would have held the ring if I'd actually been wearing it in the first place. "I only wore it at the club because Cecily asked me to. She said she wanted to make sure that men who came in there weren't getting the wrong idea..."

"She was trying to keep us apart," he said, as his eyes widened with understanding. I nodded.

"That's the only thing I can think of," I agreed, shaking my head. "It's just...I knew she wanted you, but..."

"She tried to seduce me," he admitted. I stared at him for a moment. And then it hit me. The memory of the staff gossiping about her running out of one of the playrooms. Had he been the one she was in there with? Surely not...surely she wouldn't have been that brazen.

"If she finds out you came here, she's going to fire me," I told him urgently, lowering my voice and looking around, worried that someone who might speak enough English to pick up on what we were saying was close by.

"And if it gets out that I worked at a place like that, I'm going to lose my job here, too," I continued. Even though I hadn't let the shock of all of this really sink in yet, I could hear my voice shaking. Jesus. I could lose everything if she decided to take this vendetta against me to the next level.

"You're not going to lose your job here," he assured me, and I looked up at him, wondering how he could sound so certain. But when I looked into his eyes, I believed him. I believed that he believed it, anyway, and surely that was all that mattered. Here was a man who, when the time came, had stepped up to take control for me. Who was I to say it was limited to the bedroom? Maybe I should have opened myself up to it outside of there, too.

"How do you know that for sure?" I asked, chewing my lip. He grinned at me.

"Because I'm going to buy this place."

My jaw dropped.

"I'm sorry, *what?*"

"You heard me," he replied, as though the solution should have been obvious. "I'm going to buy this place."

"I don't think that's a good idea."

"I think it is," he replied with a shrug. "Got to invest in something. And it's clear that this place isn't going to stop attracting customers anytime soon. If I want to expand my portfolio in this town, this looks like the place to do it, right?"

"And you wouldn't fire me?" I asked, feeling a little silly for even having to ask. He chuckled and shook his head.

"I wouldn't fire you."

I felt as though the ground was shifting out from under me. If what he was saying was true, then this changed pretty much *everything*. I didn't know how to wrap my head around what he was telling me right now, but I could...I could be with him. I didn't have to worry about losing my job here, about Cecily trying to smear me across town by letting slip that I had worked for her for so long.

"And I'd bump up your wages, too, so you didn't have to work with Cecily if you didn't want to," he continued. He sounded confident, calm, collected, and I wondered how he was able to just walk in here with such sureness in his heart. I wished I could approach him with the same certainty, but until this moment, I had been sure this was all a limited-time-only offer.

"But what about...us?" I asked him, lowering my voice and looking around again. The last thing I wanted was to attract the attention of anyone who might have been listening, but luckily, the universe had conspired in my favor to keep my coworkers busy in the back and my customers away for the time being.

"What about us?" he asked me. I took a deep breath. There was so much I wanted to tell him, so much I wanted to say, but I had no idea where to even start with it.

"Do we...do we keep doing this?" I pressed. I didn't know how to put the words into the form they needed to take to get across to him how much I wanted him, but I couldn't let this moment slip through my fingers. Not after everything that had happened. Not after everything we had both risked to be here. I was going to be with this man, and that was the end of it. I was going to tell him how I felt, and not let a single inch of nervousness get in the way of that.

"I would love to, if you would," he replied, simply. I felt something soften inside of me. He was so gentle, so sweet...and when it counted, he could be so completely otherwise, too. He was the perfect mix of a man I had never known I needed, and I was already obsessed with finding out just what we could mean to each other now that we had broken down the barriers that had stood between us.

"I'd like that a lot," I admitted, trying to stem the giant-ass grin that was threatening to rise up on my face. I knew I should have been more careful, but it was hard, when I just wanted to throw myself over the counter towards him and tell him I was glad, so glad that he was finally here beside me.

"But...don't you have to go back to America?" I wondered aloud. He shook his head.

"I think we should talk about this over dinner," he suggested, and I nodded with a smile. The two of us hadn't actually been out on a real date together yet, and it seemed like something of an oversight, especially if we were going to go ahead and actually do this for real.

"Agreed," I replied. "Where? When?"

"You know the Café Bernard?" he asked me. My eyes widened. I knew it, but I had never imagined in a million years someone like me might actually be able to get a table there.

"Really?" I replied, and he nodded.

"Might as well do this properly, right?" he replied, with a playful smile. Glancing around to make sure nobody was watching, he leaned over the counter, and planted a kiss on my lips. It was just a brief moment, a brief connection, but I knew it was everything I needed right now. Everything that would tell me this was right, that this was real. There was still so much we needed to figure out, but for now...he was mine. And that was all I needed to know.

"I'll see you later," he replied. "Seven?"

"Seven," I agreed, and with that, he headed out of the store and left me standing there and staring after him, a goofy-ass grin on my face. Because the man I wanted, the man I had fallen for, he wanted me back. And I couldn't think of much better in the world than that right now.

17

VICTOR

As I waited for her at the restaurant, I wondered if she was actually going to turn up. My leg was jiggling nervously under the table, and I planted a hand on it to keep it from bouncing around so much. I needed to control myself.

Besides, I knew she was going to be here. There was no way she could have faked the way she looked at me before. No way she could have made up the excitement shining in her eyes when I said I had wanted her. I had started to move in on buying the bakery, and it wouldn't be long until that place was mine. I knew everything would be easier once she could be sure she wouldn't be wrapped up in a scandal for daring to have a job not everyone approved of, but I didn't care too much. As long as she was with me, I would be here by her side to weather the storm of any scandal that came her way. And nothing was going to change that.

She appeared in the doorway, and I rose to my feet at once. She was wearing a knee-length red dress with a deep slash in the front to show off a generous amount of cleavage, and I couldn't help but smile at how beautiful she looked, her hair loose around her shoulders and her eyes glittering in the candlelight around us. The host guided her to the table, and I greeted her with a kiss on the cheek.

"You look incredible," I told her, and she beamed at me and did a little spin on the spot.

"You like it?" she asked, and I nodded.

"I love it," I replied, and I pulled out her seat for her so she could sit down, before I planted myself opposite her and just looked at her for a moment.

Hard to believe that, after everything we had been through, this was our very first date together. I felt like I already knew her far too well for that, and I knew there was so much more for me to discover about her...about the way she lived her life, about her passions, about what she loved and what she hated. But all that mattered now was that I had her to myself, and I intended to make the very most of that I possibly could.

"See, no wedding ring," she remarked, holding her hand up and twisting it back and forth to show off her bare fingers. "Nothing to worry about."

I shook my head.

"I can't believe Cecily really thought that would work," I said. She sighed.

"She really wanted you for herself," she explained. "And I don't think she was so cool on the thought of just letting you go. I kept waiting for her to jump out from behind a corner or something when I was getting ready for going out with you today, but no sign of her yet."

"Good," I replied. "Let's keep it that way. And let's not give her any more space tonight. I just want to be out with you."

"Agreed," she replied, and she smiled at me. Her smile was luminous, something that seemed to light up the whole room around us; it was a mystery to me why nobody else was turning to look at her, to see the way her gaze seemed to pull in everything else in the room. But honestly, I was glad I was the only one who seemed to have seen it. I wanted this woman all to myself. And, finally, for once...I had her just where I wanted her.

"So, can I ask you something?" she asked, once we had ordered the wine. I nodded.

"Anything."

"What about your life back in the USA?" she asked me with concern. "I know it's not my place to dig, but if...if we're going to do this, I'm not sure I can manage it with you all the way across the world. And I'm not about to give up the life I built for myself here."

"And I would never ask you to," I assured her. "I promise, I'm never going to try and get you to let go of what you have here. That's the reason I like you so much. You're not like anyone else I've ever met. You're out here, living the life you want to live, no matter what anyone else thinks of you. That's one of the most amazing things anyone can do for themselves. And I want that, too."

"So what does the life you want look like?" she asked.

"I didn't know for a long time," I admitted. "Or at least, I wasn't willing to admit what I did know about what I wanted. I knew I was never truly happy back in New York, but I didn't want to leave my family behind, I didn't want to drop them with no explanation. But I always found myself drawn back here, even when I knew I should have been working on building a life for myself back home."

I shook my head.

"But that place never felt like home to me," I admitted. "So I just kept looking for ways out. For reasons to avoid doing what everyone else around me was doing. That's why I came to invest in the winery here. I just wanted something to get me away from life back in New York. I thought it would be a good break, a chance to reset, but..."

I trailed off and shook my head again. I wasn't even sure

where I could begin in telling her all the ways this trip had totally and utterly changed my life. I wished I had the words, but I didn't, and I just had to hope she could read the sincerity inside of me right now.

"But I can see now I was wrong," I replied. "I came out here and I don't think I ever had any intention of going back when it was all over. I wanted to start again. I wanted somewhere I could call my own, and this...this place is it. I don't want to go back. I want to stay here, with you, and I want you to show me just how you made this life for yourself that you seem so happy with."

She just gazed at me for a moment, and for a second, I thought I had come on way too strong, but after an instant, she reached across the table and put her hand on mine, a warm smile spreading over her face.

"How did you know just what I wanted to hear?" she asked me softly, and she giggled as she reached for her wine. "Victor, I...I don't know what to say. When I saw you in the club, I knew there was something between us, but I didn't think..."

She just trailed off and shook her head, but she was smiling. And it was clear this was everything she had been waiting to hear from me. It might not have been how I expected any of this to go, but I wasn't going to fight it. There was something that had drawn us together. A love of this place, of this country, two people cast a long way from home and looking for adventure. And we had found it in one another. And now that we had, there was no way we were going to let it go.

We spent the rest of the night talking to one another...getting to know each other outside of the cover of bedsheets and night, of kink and whispers and sneaking around. And, just as I had guessed, she was as brilliant as I had hoped she would be. Smart, funny, charming, passionate about her baking, full of ideas about what she wanted to do in the future and ready to share each and every one of them with me. She talked with her hands as she got a little tipsy, and she made me laugh with anecdotes about her family, who she was already talking about introducing me to. I was glad to hear that. I was sure my family were going to adore her as much as I was, too. They had always loved a girl with attitude, and Lauren was, without a doubt, just that for me.

The food was delicious, the music soft and romantic, and I held her hand over the table like it was the first time I had ever been allowed to touch her. And, in a way, it felt like it was. It was the first time we had touched each other without having to worry about what might happen if someone caught us in the act, about what would happen if someone saw us together.

I was never going to let her slip through my fingers again. I couldn't say I loved her yet...too soon for that...but I felt it. We connected, on some deep and profound level.

I paid the bill. She argued. I ignored her, and she insisted on leaving the tip at least, and I fetched her coat and draped it over her shoulders so we could step out into the cool night that was waiting for us.

"Rain," she remarked, spreading her hand out in front of her. "Reminds me of the night you turned up at the club."

"Which one?" I asked her. She smiled at me.

"The one where you didn't actually get inside, let's just say that," she teased me lightly, as she looped her arm through mine. The warmth of her body against mine was enough to make me certain that all of this had been right...that being with her was everything that I had needed it to be, all this time. She was the representation of everything I had come here looking for...excitement, adventure, newness. Not to mention a damn good head for wine.

She leaned her head on my shoulder as we waited at the crosswalk, and she guided me towards a street I hadn't seen before.

"Where are you taking me?" I asked her, and she smiled at me.

"You still haven't seen my place, right?" she pointed out. "Only fair that you get a look at it now we're...well, officially doing this."

"Couldn't agree more," I replied, and I dropped a kiss on the side of her head. I was so glad I didn't have to hide from this anymore, that I didn't have to worry about getting caught. And I was never going to forget how good it felt to be with her in that moment...how good it felt to know that this woman wanted me, and to be able to tell the world at large that I wanted her, too. We were really doing this, and it was as perfect as I could have hoped.

Right up until we saw the woman waiting for us outside Lauren's apartment building. And the two of us froze on the spot.

18

LAUREN

"Cecily?" I demanded, as soon as I saw my boss standing there, soaked to the bone and shivering, outside my block.

"What are you doing here?" I asked her at once, striding towards her to make sure I hadn't managed to get her mixed up with someone else. Because there was no way in hell this could be real, could it? No way she could have found out where the hell I had been tonight. I had noticed a few waiters giving me sideways glances, but I hadn't thought anything of it. I had just wanted to enjoy my dinner and not think about who else might have been watching.

"I knew it," she spat at me, looking between the two of us with a burning rage in her eyes. "You're with him, aren't you?"

"What does it look like?" I replied, maybe a little more sarcastic than I needed to be. This was the woman, after all, who had tried to throw a monkey wrench in the works of something I had been waiting for my entire life. Forgive me if I'm not exactly oozing with patience for her, you know?

"You know that she's married, don't you?" she snapped towards Victor.

"No, she isn't, Cecily," he replied, and his voice was far

calmer than it had any right to be. If she had been talking to me like that, if I hadn't been used to it from years of working as her underling, I would have flipped my shit. But maybe he understood that he had to deal with this attitude from her for just a little while longer, and then all of this would go away.

"We talked," he replied. "We talked about everything that you've been trying to string us both along with, and we're not buying it for a second. You knew I was interested in Lauren, so you tried to institute all the rules you could to make sure I couldn't get close to her. Well, it's not going to work anymore. I know what you've been doing. We both do."

"I'll...you can't do this to me," she fired back angrily, glaring at me once more. She knew she couldn't take this out on him, not really, but she could keep trying when it came to what she felt like I had done to her. I could have pointed out that I had done nothing wrong, that I had just fallen for a single man who wanted me just the same way I wanted him, but she would have been spitting needles if she'd heard it come out of my mouth. She needed me to be the villain here, even though she must have been getting close to seeing that she was the one who took up that role.

"You don't understand," she continued. "She's not...she's just a waitress. She doesn't have anything to offer you, Victor. I do. I have the club. I have a whole reputation here."

"A whole reputation that you can't even tell anyone about because you know most people in this town would be disgusted if they found out what you did for a living," I pointed out to her. "You need to drop it, Cecily. Victor isn't interested in you. You tried your best, you didn't win. Please, get away from my house before I call the police."

"I'm giving you one last chance, Victor," she told him, completely ignoring what I was saying to her. To my delight,

Victor just laughed. It was obvious he was firmly and truly done with everything she was trying to spin this messy situation into.

"I didn't even want the first one," he replied, and the two of them stared at each other for a long moment. For a split second, I thought she was going to crack and throw herself at him right there in the middle of the street...much like she had done when she had been back at the club and tried to seduce him, by the sound of it. But instead, she drew herself up to her full height and tipped her chin slightly skywards.

"Well, I hope you know that you're not working for me anymore," she told me. I held my hands up.

"I was hoping you'd say that," I replied. "I don't want to work for you anymore, not if you're going to treat the people who basically run that place for you as if you have control over every aspect of their lives."

"And I'm going to tell everyone you worked there!" she exclaimed, as though it had just hit her that she could use it against me. I cocked my head to the side at her.

"You really think that's going to work?" I asked. "People don't care what I do to make ends meet. And besides, if you have to come out and tell people that you knew where I worked, don't you think they might wonder *why* you have such an intimate knowledge of that place? You think all your investors and all the people who support you would be happy to just go along with giving you money if they knew you were using it to fuel a place like that?"

Her jaw dropped. It might not have been fair to throw it in her face like that, but then, when the hell had this woman ever played fair with me? Why should I suddenly start respecting her, when she had tried to shoot down one of the best things that I'd ever had? I didn't want to lose this man, and I didn't want her to think for an instant she actually had any impact on my life. That would just be handing her the satisfaction I knew I could never let her walk away with.

"That's what I thought," I replied, and I turned to Victor and looked up at him with a sweet smile on my face. "Now, shall we get inside? It's cold out. I don't want you to get wet."

And, with that, we walked away from Cecily, left her standing there in the middle of the street looking as though she had just been hit by a baseball bat. Several, actually. Well, let her take some time to work out what she had just done. Let her realize she couldn't just go demanding anything she wanted, and call that a relationship. Victor wanted me, and I wanted him, and nothing she had tried to do to stop that would change the way we had turned out.

As I pushed the key into the lock, I realized my hands were shaking slightly. No matter how justified I knew I was, there was still something scary about talking back to your boss like that. Victor slipped an arm around my waist, and pressed a kiss against my neck.

"I didn't know you had it in you," he said playfully, and I smiled and snuggled against him.

"Oh, just wait 'til you see everything else that I have in me," I shot back, and I opened the door and pulled him towards the stairs. I knew this was only just starting, but I didn't care. I was falling for him, and I wasn't going to let anything at all get in the way of my enjoying the thrill of being with this man who made me feel alive in a way nobody ever had before. As soon as we reached my doorway, I paused for a moment, wondering if I was really ready to bring him inside...wondering if I was really ready to do this.

And then, he planted his lips against mine once more, and I felt something give inside of me, and I knew. I knew this was right. That it had been right from the first moment we had laid eyes on one another in that club. And I was so far beyond the point of trying to pretend anything otherwise that I couldn't hold back now that I had him here.

I pulled him over the threshold, and closed the door behind us. The rest of the world could wait. Right now, all that I cared about was having him right where I knew I deserved him.

19

VICTOR

I woke the next morning to the streaming light pouring through the window opposite her bed, and to the sound of her soft breathing as she slept next to me.

And I knew that this was how I wanted to wake up every single day for the rest of my natural-born life.

I couldn't remember every detail of what we had gotten up to the night before once we had arrived back from dinner. I could just recall that it had been a whole lot of fun, the two of us fooling around all night long, drinking some cheap wine that she had left in her cupboard before we'd dive beneath the covers once more and get lost in the thrilling sensation of what happened when our bodies came together. It wasn't even kink, at least not to any extreme degree. A little wrist-pinning here, maybe some spanking there, but just enough to remind ourselves that we were as far from boring as we could possibly be. All I had wanted from the first night we spent together as a real couple was the promise that this was going to keep going, that I wasn't going to lose her again. That she was mine.

And, as I looked over at her, her hair splayed across the pillow and her lips slightly parted as she rested, I knew I had gotten just what I knew I needed. I reached over to smooth my finger over her cheek, and she slowly opened her eyes and looked at me, as though she had almost forgotten I had actually been staying the night.

"Well, good morning," I greeted her, and she rolled on to my chest and yawned, nuzzling against me happily as she snuggled her body against mine.

"Good morning," she murmured back, and she closed her eyes and let out a long sigh once more.

"Do you have to go to work today?" I asked her, and she shook her head at once.

"I had a shift at the club sketched in, but I doubt she's going to want me there anymore," she giggled. "Good riddance, I say."

"I agree," I replied. "Let's just stay in bed all day, alright?"

"Yeah, I'm with you on that one," she agreed, and I wrapped my arms around her. She was deliciously naked under the covers, and it took everything that I had not to push her to wake up properly so I could do everything that I wanted with her. But there would be time for that later. For now, I just wanted her to rest, so she was at peace when it came time for us to make our plans for the day.

But I was wide awake. I had been since the moment I realized I was here with her, and I knew there was plenty for me to be getting on with right now. Like securing the deal at the bakery. I knew that Lauren had given Cecily a piece of her mind, and I doubted the other woman was going to try to disgrace her with news of where she used to work, but I wanted to be dead sure that Lauren never had anything to worry about as long as she was with me.

I called up my lawyers and headed into her small bathroom so I could speak to them without waking her up. This apartment was tiny, and I didn't want her to have to get up any sooner than she was ready to. She'd had a hell of a day the one before this, and I knew she was going to have to get all the rest she could to make up for it.

I didn't want to explain to them why I had decided to invest so much of my money in apparently keeping alive the food and wine sector of Brittany, but eventually, I had to come clean. One of the lawyers asked me, straight up, what I saw in a place like this, and I couldn't help but smile.

"It suits me," I explained to her. "And I want to make sure I do everything I can to keep it that way. This seems like the best way to do that."

It wasn't much, but hey, they weren't the ones making the investment, so they just went along with it and agreed they would put the offer forward to the owner of the bakery. I was certain, with the amount I was offering to throw down, that he would say yes, but it was always a gamble.

Then, hadn't everything been, since I had come out here? Everything had been a shot in the dark, and it had turned out better for me than I ever could have predicted it would. Maybe that was what I had needed…something I couldn't control, something I could just jump into without overthinking it like I always did. Lauren seemed to embody just that in the way she lived her life, and I was envious of what she had achieved because of it…and, when the time came, I knew that I would learn it from her, too. That I would learn how to live with myself, without having to control every aspect of my life, to just do what felt right because I knew it was what made sense.

When I emerged from the bathroom, I found Lauren in her small kitchen, brewing a pot of coffee. I wound my arms around her from behind and planted a kiss on her neck.

"Dare I ask what you were doing in there for so long?" she asked me playfully. I chuckled.

"Just making sure the deal with the bakery is going through," I explained. "I didn't want to wake you up."

"You're so thoughtful," she sighed happily, and she turned her head to kiss me before she handed me a mug of coffee.

"Thanks," I said, and I took a long sip. It was bitter, pitch-black, and delicious, just the way that I liked it.

"I like your place," I remarked, looking around. I really meant it. It wasn't huge, but it was clearly hers, filled with mementos of her life in this place, recipe cards tacked to the kitchen cabinets, a stack of baking supplies on the counter.

"It's your place now, too," she pointed out, and I turned to stare at her for a moment.

"What do you mean?"

"I'm not going to make you keep paying for that hotel room when you could be staying here with me," she said. "You should come stay for a while. Doesn't have to be forever. Just until you find a place."

I wasn't sure what I was hearing could actually be real, but she was talking as though it was the most obvious thing in the world. I couldn't keep the smile off my face. I knew this was crazy, and I knew that the me who had existed a few weeks before would have laughed at the idea of moving in to live with a woman I barely really knew.

But I did know her. I was tired of trying to second-guess everything, overthinking everything to the point where I might as well have just dived in and enjoyed it in the first place. I liked being with her.

I cupped her face in my hand and looked into her eyes. I couldn't believe I was even really thinking about saying this, but I didn't know how else to bring it to life. I needed her to know the truth. I needed her to hear it. I leaned my forehead against hers, and she seemed to guess what was about to come out of my mouth before I so much as said it...at least, judging by the smile on her face right now.

"I love you," I said to her. And I had been nervous before I had said those words out loud, but now that they were out there I knew they were right. I did love her. I loved what we had together. I loved what we had made, and I never wanted to let go of it.

"I love you, too," she replied, and she kissed me again, and suddenly, the coffee that she had made for me was the very last thing on my mind. I wrapped my arms tight around her and smiled against her kiss.

EPILOGUE
LAUREN

"You need to get out of bed!" Victor called to me from the bathroom, and I let out a playful groan and called right back to him.

"Wouldn't you rather come and join me?" I asked him playfully, as he emerged from the shower, dripping-wet and looking so delicious that I could hardly stand it. He cocked an eyebrow at me, and I sat up to pull him onto the bed and wrapped my arms around him.

"Come on, you have to admit, it would be way more fun to just stay in bed all day than actually go out," I said. I could already feel him giving in to me, even though he knew I was totally playing him right now. He never seemed to mind when I was playing him, as long as it came with the bonus of running late to work for all the best possible reasons.

Besides, when it came to work, it wasn't as though the two of us were beholden to the same rules as everyone else who ran the place. The bakery, well, that had been my domain for nearly a full year now, and I had made sure nobody could question my authority...well, at least not when it came to rolling in a little late, freshly fucked, and already counting down the minutes until I could get my hands on my man again, at least.

It was hard to believe I had been in charge of that place for nearly a whole year now. The sale had gone through pretty much as soon as Victor had offered the money in the first place. It seemed like the old owner was ready to move on, and just glad he wouldn't have to worry about losing cash on the place. And I was installed as the new manager at once. I kept the old staff that we'd had around, hired a few more to try to expand our savory section, and set to work making sure that nobody would ever dare say I had only gotten this place because of the man I happened to be in love with.

I thought that I had been busy before, when I had been working two jobs to make ends meet, but working full-time at the bakery was way more exhausting than I had imagined it would be. At first, at least, it took me a while to get used to the grind of getting up early every single day, making sure that our daily creations were all out by the time people had started going in to work, listening to the feedback from the customers to try to ascertain that we were delivering the very best we could. Now I started to understand why Cecily had been such a bitch. She was probably stressed out of her mind just trying to keep that place ticking over, right?

Honestly, I didn't give Cecily any space in my mind these days. Both of us had avoided the club since the blowout where I had lost my job there. Victor's friend Oliver still occasionally attended with his wife, and they said it wasn't nearly as much fun as it had been before. I joked that it was always my presence that had made the place so exciting, but honestly, maybe there was something to that. I doubted the rest of the staff would have been so pleased when they found out the reasoning behind her getting rid of me, and news traveled fast enough in this town that I was certain that they would have caught on by now.

But I didn't care about that anymore. I had the job that I had always wanted...running a bakery, getting to experiment with new recipes as well as bringing classic ones back to the forefront of our product line. We had even been asked to help cater a certain fancy old food festival, and I had been experimenting with some old recipes I had found online to bring back the taste of Brittany from a few hundred years ago.

And, of course, Victor was helping out as best he could, too, with his winery. I knew I shouldn't call it *his,* given that he just had a share in it, but since he had moved here, he had basically taken up a third-place owner position with Oliver and Natalie, who had become good friends of ours in the process. And yes, they were the kind of friends who were more than willing to test out a new bottle of wine on us, something I was always glad to help with my opinion on.

Not to mention the fact they were still involved with the kink community here. Aside from working at the club, I had never really dived into anything like that on my own terms, and honestly, I was just glad I had some people to help show me the way. Because being with Victor was amazing, even without the kinky side of it, but the kinky side just so happened to be an enormous amount of fun, too, and I wanted to learn every inch of it I could. We were constantly sneaking away for weekend trips in the big cities together, to see how people played there, getting new ideas to bring home to our own little bedroom in Brittany together.

Which, of course, was where we were right now. We kept on talking about getting a bigger place, moving out of the apartment I had lived in by myself before I met him, but we never seemed to get around to it. Even though I knew he could have afforded to buy half the city, he was happy with what we had, and there was no way I wanted to upend that. If it wasn't broken, why the hell should I go out of my way to fix it? I loved sharing this little space with him, being able to pull him straight back into bed when he had just come out of the shower, and I didn't intend to sacrifice that for the sake of some fancy place I could show off about on social media.

"You're very distracting, you know," he said to me. I grinned at him. I could already feel his hands sliding up my waist, and I knew he was going to pin me to the bed and fuck me until I begged for mercy, just the way I liked it. Sometimes, you didn't need all the toys and all the torture. You just needed one man who made you feel like you never needed to put up a fight, and everything else would just fall into place.

"Oh, am I?" I asked him, fluttering my lashes at him playfully, as though all of this was news to me. "I hope I'm not getting in the way of your day."

"You know you are," he growled in my ear, as his hands moved over my arms and pushed them down on to the bed.

"And I'm going to make you pay for it," he continued. I closed my eyes as he moved his mouth against my neck. It was always way too tempting to try to tease him, just to see what he would come up with by way of punishment. So far, they had all been a pretty damn good time, as far as I was concerned.

But no matter what he chose to do to me, no matter how much he tormented me, I knew that, when it was over, he would hold me in his arms and tell me he loved me more than anything. And he proved it, every single day that he spent with me. As I lost myself to the sweetness of his touch, I knew I had made the right choice in spending my life with him. He was what I deserved, his kindness, his support, and his total sadism whenever I asked for it. I was in love with Victor Rousso, and I knew nothing was ever going to take that away from me.

MORE BOOKS BY JESSIE COOKE

Just like Grey Novels

Just like Grey Boxsets

Just like Grey Singles

Hot Mess - A One-of-a-Kind Romantic Comedy Action Adventure unlike anything you've ever read!

All My Books including MC Romance and Bad Boys at JessieCooke.com

Copyright © Jessie Cooke

All rights reserved.

No part of this book may be reproduced in any form or by any electronic or mechanical means, including information storage and retrieval systems, without written permission from the author, except for the use of brief quotations in a book review.

License.

This book is available exclusively on Amazon.com. If you found this book for free or from a site other than Amazon.com country specific website it means the author was not compensated and you have likely obtained the book through an unapproved distribution channel.

Acknowledgements

This book is a work of fiction. The names, characters, places and events are products of the writer's imagination or have been used fictitiously and are not to be construed as real. Any resemblance to people, living or dead, actual events, locales or organizations is entirely coincidental.

Printed in Great Britain
by Amazon